THE STUNT

A BOSTON BLIZZARD NOVELLA

C.L. ROSE

THE STUNT

A BOSTON BLIZZARD NOVELLA

To all the girls who love football pants and the players that wear them.

PLAYLIST

1. Yes or No - Jung Kook

2. You Could Start a Cult - Niall Horan f. Lizzy McAlpine

3. Love U Like That - Lauv

4. You Put a Spell on Me - Austin Giorgio

5. Champagne & Sunshine - PLVTINUM, Tarro

6. Chills - Mickey Valen f. Joey Myron

7. Lights Down Low - Max

8. Falling Slowly - Vwillz

9. All In - Chri$tian Gate$

10. Something Different - Why Don't We

11. Wildest Dreams (Taylor's Version) - Taylor Swift

12. golden hour - JVKE

13. Eyes Off You - PRETTYMUCH

AUTHOR'S NOTE

When I finished writing Hot Route, I wanted to move right on to Dalton's story. I started it, but it seemed like every time I went to type, Maverick would speak up in my head. He was only mentioned once, very briefly in Hot Route, so I hadn't planned on making him a part of this series. But Maverick wouldn't shut up. When I started listening, I found a guy who was pretty simple. What you see is what you get with him, so I knew his story wasn't complex enough to become a full-length book. But I wanted to give him his HEA.

Planning this book out was pretty easy for me. I felt from their first meeting that Mav and Bella were soulmates. They didn't need any huge conflicts or drama to make their story enjoyable. That's why I felt they were perfect for a fun, fluffy, sexy novella.

I hope you enjoy this one. And rest assured that I can now get back to work bringing Dalton to his knees for the one woman that seems to be immune to his charm.

PROLOGUE

MAVERICK

"WHAT THE FUCK, ref? Are you blind?! His foot was out of bounds!" I yell, probably a little closer to the line judge than I should be. But after losing last year's AFC Championship game because of a blown call, I'm a little bit of a raw nerve. We can clinch a playoff berth with a win today and I just want to get it in the books. I have more pressing matters to attend to after the game is over.

The defense has really had to step up for this one. Our offense isn't having a great day, most likely due to whatever our best receiver, Blaze Beckham has going on. He's definitely not himself. He's been dropping passes and screwing up routes. It's been weighing on the entire offense, so I've been doing my best to hype up my guys on defense to make some big plays. Which, we have.

Coach Mills tosses the red flag he keeps tucked in his sock, challenging the ruling on the field. The refs congregate by the replay machine as we all turn our attention to the Jumbotron, where the slow-motion video begins. The receiver makes the grab, but his left toe is clearly on the line. Our fans erupt into cheers as the replay above us freezes and zooms in on the offending appendage. The zebras break apart, one of them clicking the microphone button on his belt before speaking.

"After further review, the receiver's foot was on the line. The ruling on the field of a complete pass has been overturned. Fourth down."

The cheers get louder as the defense celebrates while returning to the line. We're up by three points with fifteen seconds left on the clock. The Tennessee Bobcats are just outside of their kicker's field goal range, so all we have to do is stop them here and the Blizzard are playoff bound.

I take my spot at the end of the defensive line and put my hand on the turf, ready to take off like a rocket as soon as the ball leaves the center's hands. They have no choice but to go with a pass play here if they want a chance at getting out of bounds in order to stop the clock. They won't have enough time to get their kicking team out here if they run it. So, my job here is simple.

Get to the quarterback and fuck up his day.

The ball is snapped, and I have tunnel vision. I'm blocked by their lineman, but he's not nearly as good as I am. Spinning inward, I roll off him, seeing an open lane directly toward their quarterback. He's oblivious to me approaching as he goes through his progressions, looking for an open man. I go straight for him, aiming for his midsection as I wrap my arms tightly around him. The whistles blow and the crowd cheers as I pop up to my feet and point directly above the thirty-yard line. *That was for you, Songbird.*

The crowd goes wild as the cameras pan to the suite above, showing their very own pop princess on the

Jumbotron as she cheers like a maniac before blowing me a kiss.

Here we fucking go.

ONE
MAVERICK

One Week Earlier

I PULL my Range Rover into the parking lot behind my publicist's office. I have no idea why the fuck I'm here instead of at home in an ice bath after this week's game, but Twyla said it was a *'very pressing matter'*, so here I am. I swear if this is another one of those meetings that could've been an email, I'm taking her off my Christmas card list.

Hitting the elevator button, I almost fall asleep standing up as I make my way to the twenty-eighth floor. I've been with Overtime PR since my rookie year, and I've only been here a handful of times. I try to stay out of the media unless it's for good reasons, so it's rare that Twyla actually needs to see me. Usually, she just sends me an email with upcoming charity events and appearances, I decide which ones won't interfere with my schedule, and I do what I need to do to keep her off my back.

This is my third season playing for the Boston Blizzard and I've managed to somehow keep myself out of the limelight. It's not that I don't like the attention that comes with being a professional athlete, I just know how easily the court of public opinion can turn on you at the drop of a hat, so I try to focus on football and keep my nose clean. I've worked too hard to get where I am to get distracted by things that don't matter. It's worked well for me, so far.

The doors open and I step out of the elevator. The reception area is elegant and simple, with bright walls, white marble floors, and gold accents everywhere. People in sleek suits move around, most giving their undivided attention to their phones or tablets without even looking up.

Stepping up to the front desk, I greet the receptionist. "Hey, Henry," I say, leaning forward onto his desk and tapping my knuckles softly.

A smile spreads across his face as he stands, dapping me up. "Mav! My man!" he says excitedly. "Great game yesterday. Been trying to get you in a trade for my fantasy team, but you're a pretty hot commodity," he says, sitting back down and wiggling his mouse before typing on his keyboard.

I smirk. "Can't hear that enough."

I used to play fantasy football with my friends when I was in high school, dreaming of the day when people would choose me for their teams. It's still surreal to know that I'm living the dream I've been working toward since I first laced up my cleats in fourth grade. A lot of guys get cocky and take their place in the NFL for granted, but that'll never be me. I pour my heart and soul into every workout, practice, and game.

I hear heels clacking along the marble floors, and Twyla comes into view. She's young. Maybe in her mid-thirties, with blonde hair and blue eyes. Even with the stilettos, I still have about a foot on her. At six-five and two-hundred seventy pounds, I'm used to being the biggest guy in the room. But Twyla's personality makes me feel small as shit. The first time I met her, she told me I *had potential*. Like I was a project she was taking on out of sheer boredom. But I wasn't about to turn down an opportunity to have her as my publicist. Among some other well-known pro athletes, she also works with a slew of huge names in other areas of the entertainment industry.

"Hello, Maverick," she greets, shaking my hand with an iron grip. *Ouch, fuck.* "I'm so glad you could make it on such short notice." She motions toward her office. "Let's go talk in private."

I follow her down the hall and into the room as she shuts the door behind us. She motions for me to take a seat in one of the lush chairs situated in front of her desk as she mirrors me on the opposite side. I'm normally a pretty talkative dude, but I know when to keep my mouth shut. So, I wait for her to elaborate on why I'm here.

"So," she begins, "I called you here because I have a proposition for you." I squint, trying to figure out where this is going, but she continues. "Before I tell you what I'm thinking, are you seeing anyone?"

My eyes go wide. Does she want to date me? *Fuck.* I have a strict rule about having girlfriends during football season. I don't do it. Ever. And since I'm just not the one-night-stand type of guy, that means I usually don't have sex during that time, either. So, whatever Twyla's looking for, I'm very much *not* her guy. But how do I let her down gently? She fucking scares me.

I swallow, sweat beading down my neck. "Twyla," I start, my voice cracking like a teenager. "I don't really see you that way—"

She barks out a laugh, clutching her chest as she curls

forward. I sit and watch her, eyebrows almost touching my hairline, growing more confused by the second. "You thought *I* would date you?" she asks. Tears fill her eyes as she continues laughing, a small snort escaping her nose as she reins it in. "I don't date clients. Especially twenty-four-year-old pro athletes whose idea of romance is putting the toilet seat back down after they pee."

I furrow my brows, kind of offended because, well, *guilty.* I guess I'll work on that in the off-season.

"Anyway," she goes on. "I'd like to set you up with one of my other clients. We'll do a few public outings, get the paps to take some photos. You know, stir up a buzz. Then we can get her in a box at some of your games. The fans will go nuts for the two of you." A proud grin covers her face as she sits back in her chair.

There is no way I'm doing this. I can't have any distractions. We are a week away from hopefully clinching playoffs and the Blizzard are the favorite to win the Super Bowl. I'm also in the running for Defensive Player of the Year. All I have to do is stay focused and it's all within my grasp.

"Ummm, I can't," I say. "I mean, I don't date during the season."

She scoffs. "Maverick, you don't *really* have to date," she says, confusing me.

The imaginary light bulb above my head starts blinking as I piece together what she's saying. "You want me to like, *fake it*? For publicity?"

She nods her head. "Basically, yes. You guys can go out to dinner and maybe hold hands. Kissing would be optional. I've spoken to representatives from the NFL and they agree that this has potential to really ramp up viewership if the Blizzard makes it to the Super Bowl."

Just when I thought I understood what was going on here, I'm confused again. "What does this have to do with the Super Bowl?" I ask.

She leans forward, clasping her hands together in front of her with a cocky smirk. "Because you'd be fake dating the headliner of the halftime show."

My eyebrows just about jump off the top of my face with how surprised I am. "You want me to go out with Bella Simon?" I choke out. "As in, the biggest pop star on the planet? *That Bella Simon?*"

"Yes," she replies. "*That Bella Simon.*"

I rub my hands down my face, forcing an exhale. "Wow. Twyla. I don't know—"

She sighs loudly, cutting me off. I know when to shut up around this woman, so I stop, letting her speak. "You're the best guy for the job. You're well liked, not just in Boston, but around the entire country. You never cause trouble, rarely go out, and your dating history is harder to find than my car keys when I'm already late for work. I wouldn't ask if I thought someone else would be a better fit."

I try to find the right words to argue without sounding like an asshole, but it won't matter. She knows how to read between the lines. "Do you really think people will believe that me and Bella Simon would have anything in common? I'm a farm boy who still saves change in a jar by his bed. She's," I choose my next words carefully, "Privileged and has probably never looked at a price tag a day in her life."

She raises a dubious brow. "You think she's spoiled." It's not a question. And yes, that's exactly what I meant.

"Isn't she?" I shoot back.

Her expression softens. "You'd be surprised. Give it a chance, Mav."

I don't know why, but for some reason, I'm intrigued.

You know what? *Fuck it.*

"Okay," I say. "Set it up."

TWO
BELLA

"LET'S GO AGAIN," Sammi says, queueing up the music on her phone. We've been finalizing the choreography for the Super Bowl halftime show since about five this morning. It's after noon and I just want to get this perfect so I can grab lunch.

My dancers take their places and I step back up to the microphone, lip-synching along while they move flawlessly around me. Grabbing the mic from its stand, I walk left, into the group of dancers as I sync up with their steps. We manage to make it through the number without any mistakes, prompting Sammi to dismiss us for our lunch hour. We'll be back at it after we fuel our bodies with the sustenance we need to get through another round of grueling choreography this afternoon.

It should knock me on my ass, but after doing this since I was fourteen years old, rehearsals like this are like a second nature to me. I'm twenty-four now and I've gotten pretty good at pretending like preparing for a big perfor-mance like this is my favorite thing ever. It definitely makes things go smoother when the choreographer is happy. Sammi is kind of new to my team, but we've become pretty close in a short amount of time. People even confuse us for sisters when we go out because we share the same shade of dirty blonde hair and brown eyes. Our matching sassy attitudes are just a bonus.

I pull off my sweater, setting it down on the floor before sitting on it. Reaching for my lunch box, I unzip it and pull out the sandwich I made before I left this morning. I try my best to bring food from home when I have time to make it. Like a lot of child stars, I didn't grow up with much. My parents spent every dollar we had on opportunities for my brother and I. Bryce excelled as an actor, booking commercials before he could even speak.

But me? I can't remember ever wanting to do anything but sing. Even as a little girl, I would force my family to sit on the couch in our basement as I performed a full set-list, singing into the unplugged microphone that went with my cheap karaoke machine. I took vocal and piano lessons for hours while my friends played outside. I spent every weekend in the dance studio, learning how to move my body to perfection while other girls my age were having their first kisses. I missed out on a lot, but I was determined to make it.

When I was fourteen, I uploaded a video of myself playing the piano, singing along to Burn by Ellie Goulding. Almost overnight, my whole life changed. The video went viral and my parents' phones were blowing up with calls from people who claimed they could make me into the next big thing.

And, that, they did.

A year later, I headlined my first arena tour.

It's been ten years since I posted that video, and my life has been a dream ever since. I'll admit that sometimes, it also feels like a nightmare, but I try my best to be grateful. With all the adoring fans and lavish parties with the world's biggest celebrities, there are still some downsides. I don't even know what it's like to go on a grocery trip or drive a car without worrying about being bombarded by paparazzi. And while I love this life, and *chose* this life, I do long for normalcy sometimes. What would it be like to go out on a date without cameras being shoved in my face? What would it be like to go on a date at all?

Don't get me wrong. I've been out with guys before in a group setting. But it was almost always set up to garner attention for an album or tour I had coming up. As much as I'd love a boyfriend, it's hard to get to know someone with the whole world watching. Judging. Telling one of us the other could do better. It's just easier right now not to get involved. At least while my career is still going strong. Show business is a fickle creature. Someone new could come along tomorrow and take my place. I may as well enjoy it while I can.

As I polish off the first half of my sandwich, my phone rings from beside me on the floor. My publicist's name flashes across the screen, and I answer, still chewing. "Hey, Twyla!" I greet her cheerfully.

"How's my little pop princess today?" she practically sings. I was her very first client and although she's barely ten years older than me, Twyla is like my second mom. My parents and I had several choices when it came to PR companies, but Overtime was the only option for me. At the time, their headquarters was a two-room office that was painted in various shades of pink. I'm sure Twyla cringes at her interior design choices from back then, but they just might've been the reason I felt so comfortable with her. Fourteen-year-old girls aren't all that complex.

I breath a laugh. "Exhausted. But I'm really excited for this show."

"It's a pretty big deal," she says, pride dripping from her tone. "It's not every day you get asked to perform on national television with a hundred million people watching.

Well, *fuck me*. Could've done without that tidbit of information. No matter how many shows I do, I still get nervous.

She takes my silence as an opening. "So," she begins, her voice saccharine sweet. She definitely wants something. "Remember how we talked about stirring up some publicity before the big game?"

"Yeahhhhhh," I reply, skeptically.

"Well, I came up with the perfect plan." Twyla is always plotting, so I'm not surprised that she's concocted a scheme to create some publicity for this show. "Do you know who Maverick Moran is?"

I shake my head no, like she can actually see me before reaching into my lunch bag and pulling out an apple. "Nope," I say, taking a bite.

"He's one of my clients, as well. He plays defensive end for the Boston Blizzard. They're in a great position to make it to the Super Bowl, so the two of you could really get some attention as a couple. I think we could—"

"A couple?" I say, standing up. "What do you mean?" I really hope she isn't saying what I think she is.

"Before you say no, hear me out," she pleads.

I sit back down, blowing a loose strand of hair out of my face. "I'm listening."

She exhales a relieved breath before launching into the details. "He's a really great guy. He stays out of trouble and does all sorts of charity work. He's never been arrested, and I haven't found any scorned exes in his past."

Is it just me, or is the bar really low here?

She continues. "I'll set up some dates for you guys. The fans will go wild when they see you in public together. The wholesome football player and America's sweetheart? It's PR gold."

I can't believe she really wants me to do this. Twyla knows I've never had an actual boyfriend. My first kiss happened three years ago with one of my dancers. We decided to play Seven Minutes in Heaven when we were bored on the tour bus, and when I told him in confidence that I had never kissed anyone, he took care of me. The kiss was actually amazing, but beyond that, Darren and I have no chemistry. Which is fine because he's one of my closest friends. That's why he was also the one I went to a couple years ago when I wanted to lose my virginity. He was great with me. Very caring and attentive. But it definitely wasn't what I expected. I know I shouldn't expect mind shattering pleasure for the first time, but after the pain subsided, it was kind of just…meh. I suppose it will be better when I eventually meet a guy that I have chemistry with. But so far, that hasn't happened.

I know it seems ridiculous that I've never had a boyfriend, but I've literally been busy for the last ten years. I started recording my first album at fourteen, and I've been non-stop touring ever since. I finally decided to take some time off, but the trade with my record label and manager was that I would do this halftime show first. Once it's over, I'm going to take the rest of the year off to reset and maybe live a normal life. This summer, the label will be releasing a *Greatest Hits* album in order to keep me relevant while I'm on my break.

Bringing myself back to the present, I address my publicist. Because I have *several* questions. "I'm confused. So, you just want me to date this random football player in hopes that he makes it to the Super Bowl?"

She blows out an annoyed breath. *Sorry for asking.* "You don't have to really date. You can just fake it. It's for publicity. I promise this is a good move for the both of you. Once the game is over, we can announce an amicable break-up and you'll both move on with your lives." She says it like it's so simple. Like going out on awkward dates and pretending to like this guy is just no big deal. I've never even been on a real date. Not that this would *be* a real date. He'd be faking it the same way I would.

I take a few moments to consider everything before I make my decision. In ten years, Twyla has never steered me wrong. And it's only for a couple months. It's not like I'm going to fall in love with this guy and get my heart broken in such a short amount of time. What's the worst that could happen?

"Okay, I'll do it."

THREE
BELLA

I LOOK out the window of my private jet, legs bouncing a million miles a minute. It's a very short flight from New York to Boston, but every minute will count when it comes to Maverick and I getting to know one another. I'm so nervous. After my conversation and eventual surrender with Twyla yesterday, we set up a private meeting with him for tonight because he has a late practice tomorrow. I didn't want our first meet up to be in public because I know it's going to be awkward. At least, I know *I* am going to be awkward. Little Miss Never Had a Boyfriend. That's me. And this guy is hot. I couldn't Google him fast enough last night and I'll admit that he's one of the most gorgeous guys I've ever seen. He's got light brown hair that's perfectly messy, even after he takes his helmet off. His deep brown eyes have me sucked right into every photo. He's definitely not shy about his body, either. Every picture of him during practice has him in a tight compression shirt, abs peeking out from the bottom, and short shorts. The man's thighs are bigger than my waist.

So, not only am I going to have to deal with the general

awkwardness of talking to a guy, but said guy is sexy as hell.

The plane lands and I walk down the stairs, heading right toward my waiting car. I shiver from the chill in the air as I make my way across the asphalt. I hop in the back seat and scroll through TikTok as the driver brings me to the place I will officially meet my new fake boyfriend. Well, he isn't my fake boyfriend yet, but I know Twyla is hoping we'll see this thing all the way through to Super Bowl. For some strange reason, I'm all for it. It might feel good to do normal things that a girl my age would do. He might not actually really like me, but I can pretend that a guy like Maverick Moran would give me his time and attention.

I look out the window and notice it has begun raining. The cold Boston temperatures aren't much different than the ones in New York City, but it is especially chilly tonight, making the rain freeze slightly before it pelts the windshield with a small *thunk*.

Before I know it, we're pulling up to a high rise right in the middle of Boston. I wonder if this is where he lives. The driver takes an underground tunnel into a parking garage, where he stops in front of a revolving glass door. As I look out, confused as to what I'm supposed to do next, a tall man with wide shoulders comes into view. Holy shit, his arms look like tree trunks.

Wait. Is that...oh my God, that's *him*. I swallow thickly, completely frozen as the driver rounds the car to open my door. I'm still not moving as Maverick steps up and reaches his hand out for me to take.

RIP: Bella Simon. She died doing what she loved. Staring at the perfect male specimen while imagining him removing her clothes with his teeth.

He looks at me, still holding out his hand with his brows raised. Oh, shit. He's waiting for me. By the grace of God, I pull myself together enough to put my small hand in his large one, allowing him to gently pull me from the back seat. Tingles make their way up my arm as he laces our fingers together. I look around for cameras, but there are none.

"Hi, Bella. I'm Maverick," he says with a voice smoother than butter. My cheeks immediately blush as I look for the words to respond. Up close, I realize no photo could ever do him justice. His skin is a warm tan, even in the midst of a Boston winter. His eyes are such a deep brown, I can barely tell where the irises end and the pupils begin. And his lips are plump and kissable.

Shit. I'm in trouble.

"Umm, hi," I say shyly, pushing my hair behind my ear. If he noticed my gawking, he doesn't say so as he leads me through the door. Our bodies brush against each other as we walk, eliciting a warm feeling all the way to my core. He greets the doorman and gives the elevator attendant a high-five as we settle inside. We ride to the top floor, my hand still in his, and the door opens directly inside his penthouse apartment. Holy fuck, this is nice. I read that he was the highest paid defensive end in the league, but he renegotiated his new contract so the team had more money to give to other players. He's obviously still doing well for himself.

We step into what looks to be a decent sized foyer. The place is so clean, I can't believe a human being actually lives here. "I hope it's okay that I had you dropped off here," he begins, his brown eyes holding my attention as he lets my hand go. If I were more confident, I would reach back out for him, but I'm me, so I don't. I can't seem to look away from him as he continues. "I figured we should take a couple nights to get to know each other before we go out to public places together. It's kind of an awkward situation, so I thought we could get more comfortable with each other, so things look more natural."

Thank God this whole situation is awkward for him, too. Now I don't feel so bad.

He motions for me to sit on the couch. I do, and he sits in the chair opposite the sleek, glass coffee table.

"That's a really good idea," I say. "It's definitely not a conventional way to start a relationship—" I catch myself. "I mean, a *fake* relationship," I rush out my correction.

His eyes meet mine, and for the life of me I can't read him. "Yeah," he says, clearing his throat. "Can I get you something to drink?"

"I'll take a water, please," I reply quietly. I wish I had more confidence. I'm sure the girls he normally dates have no problem telling him what they want. I can command a stage in front of a hundred thousand people, but I'm here alone with this gorgeous man and I can't find two words to put together.

He leaves the room, returning moments later with a bottle of water. I twist off the top, gulping half of its contents in one go. That was a little cringey, but my mouth feels like the Sahara. As I lower the bottle, I look up through my lashes to find Maverick staring at me intently.

"What?" I ask. It's not making me uncomfortable like it probably should be, considering he's a stranger and I'm in his house, but I wonder what he's seeing right now. I don't have to wait long to find out.

"You're beautiful," he says, making me suck in a quiet gasp. I'm used to getting complements thrown at me, but coming from him, it's just so…intimate. A throb begins to pulse somewhere deep inside me as I fall back into his deep brown eyes.

"Thank you," I say quietly. He's definitely affecting me in a way I've never felt before. But I stop on a dime when my brain reminds me that this is all fake to him. He's saying these things in private, so it seems more natural when we get into public.

It's okay to be a little delulu and pretend like he isn't faking though, right?

Right?

"So," he says, breaking my thoughts. "Tell me about yourself." *Ugh.* I hate this part. Although it seems like I live this amazing life, I'm far from interesting. All I do is work. On the rare occasion that I have time to go out, it's set up by my team to ensure that my every move is documented by the media. And those *friends* you see me in photos with? Not really my friends. They're all there for the same reason I am. Someone told them it would further their career. That's why it should be easy for me to remember that Maverick isn't really into me. Although, by the way he's staring into my soul as he waits for my answer, I'll be needing several reminders tonight.

"There's not really much to tell," I say, fidgeting with my water bottle. "I grew up in California, but I moved to New York City with my family while I was recording my first album. My brother, Bryce, is an actor, but he's been in Italy for the past two years." I stop to think. "Sorry," I say. "I'm really not that special. I work, eat, and sleep."

He studies me for a moment before speaking. "Well, you're definitely wrong. You *are* special," he says softly. My eyes follow him as he moves from the chair to the couch, lowering himself down only inches from me. I can almost feel a ghost of a touch when his knee comes close to brushing mine. I wish it would. I smile up at him as we both turn in toward one another, getting more comfortable.

"What about you?" I ask. For some reason, I want to know every detail about him.

He blows out a breath. "Well, I grew up on a farm in Nebraska. I was offered a full scholarship to play football at the University of Miami, then got drafted to the Blizzard my senior year. And here I am."

I already knew all of that because I shamelessly Googled the fuck out of him yesterday. I want juicier details. Feeling a little braver, I ask the question I really want to know. "Any recent girlfriends?"

"Not really," he replies. "I usually have a rule about dating during the season. And before that, I went out with a few girls, but nothing serious came of it."

Twyla told me he tries to keep his personal life out of the media as much as he can. That's probably why I haven't seen many photos of him with women. A pang of jealousy hits me at the thought of him sharing an intimate, private evening with someone else. *We'll just set that aside to unpack later.*

"What about you? Any exes I need to worry about?" He smiles and I can't help but snort at the question.

"Nope," I say. "I haven't had time to date in the last ten years. You'll actually be my first."

His smile falls, a shocked expression taking its place. "You've never been on a *date?*"

God, this is so embarrassing. "Uh-uh," I say, shaking my head. I may as well just lay it out on the line for him. He's going to find out sooner or later. I exhale, trying to build up the courage to tell him how pathetic my life is, despite what the world thinks. "I've never had a boyfriend. And I've only kissed one person. He's one of my dancers and I'm pretty sure he only did it because he felt sorry for me." I look down, picking at my fingernails. I can't look at him. He probably thinks I'm such a loser now.

"Well, that won't do," he says. *Yep, he thinks I'm a loser.* I wait for him to tell me this won't work between us. That my inexperience isn't something he's willing to work with. But instead, he grabs my hand, prompting me to look at him. He brings his other palm to my face, gently cupping my cheek. "Is it okay if I kiss you?"

My eyes go wide. "What?"

He swallows, his Adam's apple bobbing, and I can't help but follow the movement. I want to put my lips on it. I want to taste his skin. "You deserve to know what it's like to be kissed by someone because they *want* to kiss you."

My breath hitches. "You want to kiss me?"

"Really fucking bad," he says, eyes on mine as he moves in just slightly.

"Okay," I whisper, leaning into his palm.

A second later, he presses his lips to mine. My eyes are closed, but fireworks explode behind them as his tongue ghosts over my bottom lip. I let out a soft moan as I open for him. His hand slides back into my hair, holding my head still as he pushes his tongue into my mouth. That sets something off inside me. I reach forward, fisting the soft fabric of his Henley as we deepen the kiss even further. I can feel his hard muscles flexing under my hand and my panties become almost unbearably wet. *Who am I?* If this is what kissing him is like, I can't imagine how good it would feel to have sex with him. Not that I'll ever find out.

My thighs clench together on their own accord, trying

to dull the ache that's growing between them. Just as I start to debate climbing him like a tree, he ends the kiss, nipping at my bottom lip once before sitting back. "You taste incredible, Bella," he rasps.

Oh Lord Baby Jesus, help me.

I'm speechless as I bring my fingertips to my lips, finding that they're swollen and tingly. I can say with one hundred percent confidence that none of this happened when I kissed Darren. If anything, I felt regret with him. But with Maverick, I want more.

He looks down at me. His hands are fisted in his lap, and I can see the muscle in his jaw tick with how hard he's clenching it. Fuck. Maybe *he's* having regrets.

"I'm sorry," I rush out.

His brows pinch. "What are you sorry for?" he asks.

I want the floor to swallow me whole. My eyes return to my abused nail beds, and I swallow, trying to moisten the dryness in my throat. "You didn't like it. I'm not a good kisser."

His cheeks fill with air before he forces out an exhale. "Is that what you think? That I pulled away because you're a *bad kisser*?"

Yes. No. I don't know. I may be a grown woman, but I'm new at this.

"You just look like you wish you could take it back," I whisper. "Your body language. It—"

"This is me restraining myself, Bella. I'm trying to be a gentleman. I'm trying to stick to the plan. You've been here less than an hour and I'm already thinking of all the ways I want to make you scream for me."

My brows shoot up. "Oh."

He sits up straight, grabbing my hands to stop me from picking at them. "Look at me."

I obey his command, snapping my eyes up to his. His expression has softened, making all the nervousness and tension in my body slowly melt away. How the hell have I just met this guy, yet I feel safer with him than I have with anyone else in my whole life? This is bad.

It's not real, Bella. It's a PR stunt. That'll be my mantra until after the big game. It's the only way I'll be able to keep my head on straight.

"I know this is supposed to be fake," he says. Oh, good. We're on the same page. "But maybe it wouldn't hurt to keep practicing. You know, for appearances and stuff. Nobody's going to believe we're together if we kiss like two dead fish." He smiles, looking down at our joined hands before bringing his gaze back up to mine. "Plus, I really like kissing you."

Mustering up all the confidence I can, I lean forward and kiss him again. This time, it's completely unhurried as we explore each other. I just about come off my seat when he uses his tongue to massage mine. God, he's good at this.

Just then, a loud screech fills the air, making us pull away from each other abruptly. Maverick fishes his phone out of his pocket and reads the alert to himself before relaying it to me. "There's a severe thunderstorm warning in effect until ten a.m. Freezing rain, high winds, and dangerous travel conditions."

Shit on toast. I hate thunderstorms. And I'm supposed to be on a plane back to New York in a couple of hours.

I sigh. "I think I'll have to get a hotel room for the night. I'm sure they aren't letting people fly out in this." I cringe as I realize what a spectacle this will be. The last time I had an impromptu overnight stay in L.A., one of the workers livestreamed me getting on the elevator. There was a mob outside within minutes. Some of them even got arrested for trespassing. I have a team of bodyguards, my driver being one of them, but this would be too much for them on short notice. Plus, only one of them made the trip. Carlo is probably at a nearby café waiting for me to text him to come pick me up.

"I don't know how I'm going to do this without people finding me," I say.

Seeing my discomfort, Maverick turns to me. "You could stay the night," he offers.

I consider it for a moment. I'm safe here. The building has excellent security, otherwise Carlo would've never left me. As awkward as it may be sleeping and waking up under the same roof as Maverick, I can't say there's anywhere else I'd feel safer if I'm not able to be at home. I certainly won't rest in a random hotel room by myself. We'll just have to deal with all the post-make out morning weirdness when we get there.

"Okay."

FOUR
MAVERICK

I'VE BEEN LYING in bed for hours and haven't slept a single second. I'm too wound up with Bella in the guest room down the hall. My dick is just about punching through my sweats with how hard it gets every time I think about her soft lips on mine, but I refuse to take care of myself. It's fucking weird. I'm a grown man, not a teenage virgin. I shouldn't even be considering jerking off to the thought of making out with Bella. Plus, if she heard me, I'd have to grow a beard, change my name, and leave the fucking country. *Not happening.*

I've spent the last hour with my AirPods in, listening to her music in the dark. I've heard the stuff that gets played on the radio plenty of times, but there are so many more songs. And they're all fucking phenomenal. The faster music is fun, but when she really gets to belt those lyrics out in the ballads? *Fuuuuck me.* She reminds me of the songbirds back home on our farm. I used to sit outside after a long day of baling hay, listening to them sing. I never knew how they did it, but their effortless melodies calmed me. Just like Bella's do.

I take out my AirPods, replacing them in their case before kicking my foot out from under the duvet, hoping the cool air will help me sleep. The rain is still pelting against the window as I lay here in silence. Just as I try to close my eyes, a loud crack of thunder followed by a blood-curdling scream have me jackknifing up and rushing out the door. I run as fast as I can to the guest room and rip open the door, finding Bella curled up in a fetal position, shaking like a leaf. I make a beeline for her, sitting on the bed and putting my hand on her shoulder. "Bella, are you okay?"

She continues trembling as she looks up at me with tired eyes. "Maverick?" She's disoriented, which makes sense. She was just ripped from a peaceful sleep by a loud noise, to find herself in a strange room.

"You're okay. I'm right here," I say softly, trying to calm her. "There was some thunder and I heard you scream, so I ran in here to make sure you weren't hurt."

She sits up, eyes wide with embarrassment. "Oh my God, Mav. I'm so sorry I woke you up."

All she did was shorten my name, but hearing her call me Mav makes my heart squeeze inside my chest. I shake it off, focusing on her. "No, you didn't wake me," I reassure her. "I couldn't sleep."

She's stopped shaking and she slowly lays back down with her head on the pillow. I can't seem to pull myself away from her, so I stay right where I am, rubbing soothing circles with my thumb on the inside of her elbow. Eventually, she speaks.

"When I was nine, we had a really bad storm. High winds, rain, thunder, lightning…the whole thing. One minute I was asleep, the next, I heard a loud crash and the tree from outside my bedroom window was just feet from me. If it weren't for the beams in the ceiling, it would've killed me. Ever since then, I have trouble sleeping through storms."

Holy shit. I can't even imagine how scary that was for her as a child. I'm thankful that her life was spared, because although I know this is supposed to be fake between us, there's something about her that has me completely captivated. She's special. And I'm glad that Twyla's crazy idea brought us together.

"What can I do to help?" I ask. I don't know why, but I feel an overwhelming urge to protect Bella. I want to make her feel safe when she's with me. I want her to know I'd never let anything or anyone get to her. I don't think she has many people like that in her life.

She lets out a breathy laugh. "After it happened, anytime it would rain, my whole family would grab their blankets and pillows and we'd all sleep together in the living room. It's silly because I wasn't in any less danger just because I was in another room, but not being in a bed right near a window helped me feel better."

I stand from the bed, reaching out my hand for her to take. "Come on," I say with a grin.

She sits up, putting her soft palm in mine, allowing me to pull her up. "Where are we going?"

"To the living room," I tell her. "I've got a million pillows and blankets. We can make a little fort on the floor and if it's okay with you, I'll sleep next to you. I'll protect you all night.

She stares at me, and although there isn't much light in the room, I can see her eyes filling with tears. *Fuck*. I didn't want to make her cry. "Hey," I say softly. "It's okay. Don't cry." I pull her into my arms as she melts into me, her small arms wrapping tightly around my waist.

"I'm sorry," she says. "I don't know what's happening to me. It's so stupid because we just met and this is all for the cameras, but I feel safer with you than I ever have with anyone else. Not my family, not my bodyguards...is that weird?"

I pull back just enough to look down at her. "It's not weird at all. You shouldn't have to go through these things alone, Bella. I'm glad you feel that way with me." I pull her close again, kissing the top of her head before turning to grab the pillows and blankets from the bed. We walk, hand-in-hand, to the living room where I lay everything out neatly on the floor before walking down the hall to my room. I take all the pillows and blankets from my bed, returning to find Bella sitting with her back against the bottom of the couch. She's so fucking pretty, I can hardly look away.

"Up for a second," I tell her. She stands, plopping on the couch while I continue to throw more blankets and pillows onto our makeshift bed. When I'm satisfied with the level of comfort it should give her, I quickly move toward the kitchen, returning to Bella with a bottle of water. "Can you drink a little for me?" I ask. What she just went through in the guest room was pretty intense and I want to make sure she feels taken care of.

Thankfully, she takes the bottle, sipping gingerly as she relaxes into the plush cushions of my wrap-around sectional. "I think I'm wide awake now," she giggles. Her eyes look tired, but I'm sure she's running on some of the leftover adrenaline from earlier.

"Okay," I say, sitting down next to her. "Wanna make out?" I give her a boyish grin, hoping that I can at least lighten the mood. I don't actually expect her to agree, but when she bites her lip and gives me a tight nod, I'm on her in an instant. I feel like it's been ages since I've felt her lips on mine, even though it's barely been a couple hours. I swallow every one of her moans as she lets me push my tongue inside, brushing it against hers. I could kiss her forever. And if she lets me, I just might.

BELLA

Holy fuck, I hope he never stops kissing me. Honestly, making out with Maverick Moran is a spiritual experience. I feel like I need to hold onto something so I don't float away as his tongue expertly teases me.

He pulls back so that he can speak, but his lips are still ghosting over mine. "Is it okay if I touch you?" he asks, a tinge of hopefulness veiling his request. "I'll stay above your clothes. I just feel like I have to put my hands on you."

I can't think of anything I want more than for this man to put his hands all over me, but I don't want to sound too eager, so I answer him with a slow nod. He immediately takes my mouth again, his hands skating down my arms, leaving a trail of goosebumps in their wake. My whole body feels like it could combust at any moment as he grips onto my waist and pulls me to straddle him. I've never been in this position with a guy before, clothed or not. Darren and I were all business when we had sex, never leaving the missionary position. So, I can't say I'm not nervous to be hovering over Maverick like this right now.

"Is this okay?" he asks, settling his hands on my thighs.

My whole body is trembling as I squeak out my affirmation. I lean forward, resting my forehead against his as I try to calm myself. My hormones are telling me to grind down on him, but I'm not sure if he wants that. He must notice my internal battle, because he pushes me back just enough to look at me straight on.

"Bella, we don't have to do any of this if you're not comfortable. We can just keep kissing until you're sick of it." He smiles. *Please.* Like I could *ever* get sick of kissing him. "I don't want you to feel like you have to do this stuff with me. It's not part of the deal."

"I want to," I rush out. I'm almost embarrassed at how desperate I sound. But when I look at him, I see the same thing. He wants whatever I'll give him. I'm having a hard time with the fact that I'm painfully inexperienced. "But I don't really know what to do." My heart is beating so hard and fast, but I wasn't lying. I do want to continue fooling around with him. Even if it is just to practice for when we're in public. The more comfortable we are together, the less awkward we'll look in front of cameras.

"Are you a virgin?" he asks. He doesn't say it condescendingly. It wouldn't be far-fetched to assume that I was, considering I did tell him I've only kissed one person earlier tonight.

"No," I reply, shaking my head. "The dancer that I kissed. I asked him to take my virginity a couple years ago. He did, but we never did it again. We're such good friends, and it was just weird. I'm not sure it's supposed to feel like that." There. It's all on the table.

His grip on my thighs tightens. "Did he hurt you?" he says, trying to remain calm. I can see the vein in his forehead beginning to pop out. *Is he jealous?*

I shake my head. "No. Well, I mean, it hurt at first. But then, it was just...nothing." I honestly can't think of a better description. It wasn't bad, but it wasn't good. It was just *nothing.* "It wasn't how the books I read make it out to be." I shrug.

"Did he make you come?" He catches me off guard and I gasp. I'm not used to talking about this stuff with anyone. Do I have toys that I use to get myself off when I'm on the road? Absolutely. But I definitely don't discuss it with anyone. Let alone a hot football player while I'm straddling his lap. I want to curl up in a ball right here. I'll never recover from this embarrassment. But what's that saying? *Go big or go home,* right?

"No, he didn't," I say quietly.

A look of mischief takes over his expression. It's equal parts panty-melting and terrifying. "Have you ever made yourself come, Bella?"

Actually, I'm about to right now. Standby.

"Y-yes."

Heat clouds his expression. I'm practically dying of embarrassment and horniness while sitting here. I don't know if I should climb off of him or not. But he makes the decision for me as he starts moving me back and forth along his lap. "I want to make you come. Is that okay?" he asks.

Oh my God. Is this really happening? I've gone the last twenty-four years of my life never being in a position like the one I am now, but I've known Maverick for like, a few hours and I'm already about to beg him for whatever he'll give me.

You know what? Fuck it. I never do anything for myself.

I nod my head, giving him the green light, but that's not good enough.

"I'm going to need your words, Bella. Tell me what you want."

And therein lies my struggle. I'm a people pleaser. When someone asks me to do something, I do it. I have no problem taking direction, but giving it is a whole different story. I always feel like a burden. Like I'm inconveniencing people by asking them to do things for me. So, I generally just end up doing whatever it is by myself. Why do I feel like Maverick can read me so well when the people who have known me all my life look at those same attributes as me being 'strong and independent'?

I take a deep breath. This thing between us isn't real, so I shouldn't worry about disappointing him. I should just tell him what I want.

"Say it and it's yours," he says, leaning in but never touching his lips to mine. We just sit there breathing each other in for a moment before I finally give in.

"I want you to make me come, Maverick." I whisper it so quietly; I don't know if he even hears me at first. But then, he slowly brings his lips to mine while he begins rocking my body back and forth over his hardening erection. It takes me a moment to surrender to the pace he's set, but when his length rubs perfectly against my clit, I relax completely and let him take control. I moan into his mouth as I feel the coil of warmth start to tighten in my stomach. My arms are wound around his neck as if I'm hanging onto him for dear life. Which, I certainly feel like I am.

He breaks the kiss and looks down to where I'm riding his lap. "Look at you. You're doing so good asking for what you want. Are you going to come for me, Songbird?"

Songbird. That nickname does things to me. I feel myself ruining my panties, and maybe even my pants, as I get wetter and wetter for him. I feel like a rubber band that's being pulled to its limit. I'll snap at any moment. I can't form words, so I just nod my head frantically as my release barrels toward me. When he leans in and sucks the sensitive skin below my ear, I go off like a rocket.

"Mav—," I choke out. "I'm coming."

"Yeah, you are. You're such a good girl. I want all of it. Soak my lap, sweetheart."

I had no idea dirty talk was a kink of mine, but I guess I never had the chance to find out what I liked. His mouth is going to be the death of me. And what a way to go.

I ride out my orgasm as Maverick stills below me, holding my hips in place as his jerk up into me. He lets out a low growl and, *oh my God, is he coming?* I look down to see that his lap is, in fact, soaked. I'm not sure if it's from me, him, or a mixture of both of us, but I love the way it looks.

I'm still shaking as he cups my cheek in his palm and presses a gentle kiss to my lips. "You're fucking incredible, Bella," he breathes. We both just sit there, my head on his shoulder, completely satiated for several minutes. Finally, I sit up and slowly move off of him, doing my best to right my clothes. But the uncomfortable wet spot on my pants is not nearly as hot as it was five minutes ago.

Seeing my uneasiness, Maverick chuckles. He stands and points his thumb toward the hallway. "I'll go grab you something to change into. You can use the bathroom down here if you want to clean up."

I try to push away the awkwardness I'm feeling, but it's in vain because my thoughts are all over the place. He takes off toward the bedroom as I make my way down the hall. I walk into the bathroom, shutting the door quietly before removing my leggings and underwear, which are both soaked, inside and out. So, it *was* a mixture of us both. I made Maverick Moran come by grinding on his lap. For a moment, I let myself feel powerful. Like I'm a sexual goddess who takes what she wants.

I'm broken from my fantasy by his quiet knock on the

door. "I have some boxers and sweatpants for you," he says. I open the door just enough to put my hand through, not wanting to see his face yet. I've definitely never had to deal with this type of situation before. If he was my boyfriend, I could probably navigate this. I could go out there wearing his clothes and be all cute on our little blanket mountain. But he's *not* my boyfriend. This is all fake. So, what's the protocol? Do I go out, thank him for the orgasm, and go to sleep? Or do I act normal, like that didn't just happen?

I change into his clothes, which are about five sizes too big. Thank God for drawstrings, because these pants would be on the floor if they weren't cinched within an inch of their life. I take one last look at myself in the mirror, fixing my disheveled hair, and rolling up my pants and underwear. I can put them in my purse and take care of them at home.

Making my way back out to the living room, I see Maverick has also changed. He's now wearing a pair of basketball shorts and a crisp, white t-shirt. *This shit should be illegal.* He makes his way to the spot he made up for us, laying down before patting on the soft, fluffy layers next to him. I wordlessly move toward him, settling in on the pillows as he wraps his arms tightly around me, pulling my body into his. Even with thunder crashing in the distance, I drift off to sleep peacefully before I can even go through all the thoughts in my head about what just happened.

FIVE
MAVERICK

I POUR the pancake batter onto the griddle and watch as little bubbles form on the surface. Normally, I would throw some random shit into the blender with my protein powder, but a smoothie is out of the question this morning. Bella is still asleep and I don't want to wake her with the loud noises my blender makes. So, Peppermint Mocha Power Cakes, it is. My teammate Blaze insists that the pumpkin ones are superior, but everyone knows the Christmas flavors are the best.

I was finally able to sleep last night after Bella laid down next to me on the floor. I wasn't sure how she'd react when I pulled her into me, but I'm glad she didn't tell me to go fuck myself. I was worried that, with everything that went down on the couch, she'd need time to process. I certainly didn't expect things to go that far, but it was like all the rational thoughts left my body as soon as my hands gripped her thighs. All I could focus on was making her feel good and showing her how a man *should* treat her. Fuck, it was the hottest moment of my life when her orgasm hit. As soon as she told me she was coming, there was nothing I could do to stop myself from busting in my pants like a goddamn teenager.

Even after everything, Bella actually seemed more relaxed with my arms around her. I didn't let go of her until I woke up, even though I'd have been happy to hold her until she told me to stop. But my raging morning wood made itself painfully known, so I had no choice but to pull away from her. As hot as last night was, I'm not dumb enough to assume Bella would want to do anything like that again. I'll chalk it up to her trying to get comfortable with me, so we look like a real couple in front of the media. And maybe the adrenaline from being so scared by the storm.

I turn off the griddle, moving all the Power Cakes to a platter just as I hear quiet footsteps enter the kitchen. Bella looks just as stunning as she did when she arrived last night, only now, she's wearing her cropped t-shirt with my sweatpants.

Goddamn.

"Morning," she yawns. She's fucking adorable, all sleepy and warm looking. I want to scoop her up, bring her to my bed, and hide under the covers until someone comes banging on the door.

"Hey," I say. "Sleep well?"

She nods her head, a shy smile blooming on her face. "I'm really sorry about last night. That was so stupid."

I go still. She regrets what we did. Fuck. Kissing her the first time was already pushing my luck. Next thing I knew, we were back on the couch a couple hours later and she was coming on my clothed cock. This is supposed to be fake. I pushed too hard and now she's having second thoughts.

She sits on one of the barstools and sighs, resting her chin in her palm. "You'd think I'd be over it after all these years. But I still wake up screaming every once in a while. I hope you were able to get to sleep okay on the floor."

Oh. She wasn't talking about what happened on the couch. Relief floods my system, making my tense muscles relax. I don't know what I'd do if she had regrets from the last twelve hours. I know I don't.

"I slept great," I tell her. "And it isn't stupid. You went through something traumatic. It's normal to still feel nervous about it. But I promise, when you're with me, you're safe."

She rewards me with a soft smile, and it takes momentous amounts of self-control not to walk over and press my lips to hers. She's so fucking pretty. But I don't want to push my luck, so I turn, plating our breakfast and setting a plate in front of her. "These smell amazing," she says, cutting off a small piece of pancake and popping it into her mouth. The moan that leaves her has my dick entering the chat. *Nope. No more, my guy. You almost got us in trouble once already.* "Okay, what are these and where can I buy them in bulk?" she asks, covering her mouth as she speaks.

I laugh, "They're called Power Cakes. They're basically just pancakes, but they have a lot of protein and they're better for you." I cut a large bite from mine, shoving it into my mouth. I chew and swallow before speaking again. "You can only get this flavor around the holidays, so I binge on them while I can."

She cuts another piece. "I'm going to need these every time I spend the night," she says. The surprised look on my face has her pausing. "I mean, if you want me here again," she adds.

God, I want her here all the time.

"I think that can be arranged," I wink, which earns me another smile before we finish our breakfast and go our separate ways.

SIX
BELLA

BELLA: What's your favorite color?

MAVERICK: What? Why?

BELLA: You're my boyfriend, duh. I should know your favorite color.

MAVERICK: Hmm. I don't remember you asking me to be your boyfriend. No flowers, no teddy bear...just an assumption? I thought we had something special, Songbird.

BELLA: *rolls eyes* OMG. Maverick Moran, will you please be my fake boyfriend?

MAVERICK: Dunno. I need some time to think about it.

BELLA: *rolls eyes HARDER*

MAVERICK: OK, since you asked so nicely. Yes, I'll be your fake boyfriend.

MAVERICK: Blue. What's yours?

BELLA: Glitter.

MAVERICK: Your favorite color is glitter?

BELLA: Yep. What's your favorite food?

MAVERICK: That depends. Do calories count?

BELLA: Nope. You can eat whatever you want and never gain a pound...what are you picking?

MAVERICK: Peanut Butter M&Ms. Bags and bags of them.

BELLA: Great choice.

"WHO'S GOT you smiling like that, boo?" Sammi asks, making me throw my phone like it's on fire.

"Jesus, Sam! You scared me," I say as I bend down and pick up my phone to find several cracks in the screen. *Fuck a duck.*

She scoffs. "I've literally been trying to get your attention for five minutes," she says. "Who are you texting that's got you so out of it?"

I talked to Twyla after I left Maverick's house yesterday and we decided that we wouldn't come out and tell anyone we were dating until after we've been seen together in public for the first time. We want speculation without confirmation for a little while. I consider Sammi to be one of my closest friends, so it's hard lying to her. "It's nobody. Just a guy." I shrug, like the thought of him doesn't stir up butterflies in the pit of my stomach.

She gasps, "A *guy?* Like, a male human? With a real penis?"

I laugh. "I mean, I haven't seen it or anything, but it would be safe to assume he has one." I *haven't* seen it, but I definitely know it exists. Flashes of dry humping Maverick on his couch until we both came play back in my mind, causing a dull throb to bloom between my legs. How do people live like this? He barely touched me and all I can think about is how badly I need more. I can't imagine the kind of animal I'd turn into if I actually had sex with him.

"And you're not going to tell me who it is," she states. "Fine. Keep your secrets. But I *will* find out." I don't doubt it. If being a choreographer doesn't work out, Sammi definitely has the skills to become an internet sleuth.

She walks away just as my dancers arrive, setting their bags down in the corner. "Hey, guys!" I say cheerfully as I drop down into a sitting position, extending my right leg to stretch. They greet me back, as usual, but I notice that Darren and Isla are sitting much closer than they normally do. I act like I'm in my own little world as he reaches out, tucking a piece of hair behind her ear as she smiles affectionately at him. Even though we agreed that we were better as friends, I've always felt a small pang of jealousy watching him give his attention to other girls. I wait for that feeling to come over me as he says something to make her laugh, but it never comes.

All I can think about is how I already miss hanging out with Maverick. The way things just happened so easily between us was refreshing. Although it was awkward talking to him at first, I ended up feeling comfortable enough to confide in him about some of my past experiences; none of which he judged me for. And as for the physical part? I didn't know because I had nothing to compare it to at the time, but when Darren kissed me, it was nothing like the way it had felt with Maverick. Everything with him made me want more. It's going to be almost impossible not to get addicted to him while we're doing this.

Even texting him the past twenty-four hours has been fun.

I stand up, ready to get this rehearsal over with. For the first time in a long time, I have something to look forward to that isn't work.

SEVEN
MAVERICK

"YOU READY TO DO THIS?" I ask Bella. We're sitting in the back of the car that Twyla sent, on the way to Donatello's for the dinner she set up for us. She's been hard at work, getting the rumor mill churning. Earlier this week, photos of Bella leaving my building *mysteriously* turned up online, causing both of our fandoms to lose their minds. People are speculating that we're dating, and it's all going exactly as planned.

"I'm nervous," she sighs. She's picking at her finger-nails, definitely a coping mechanism of hers, so I grab her hand and intertwine our fingers. Her eyes meet mine and I notice the trepidation that's clouding her expression. "What if they don't believe us? What if I screw up and everyone finds out how pathetic I really am? That I can't even get a guy to go out with me unless it's a publicity stunt? I can't—"

I shut her up by grabbing her face and crushing my lips to hers. Her body relaxes as she melts into the kiss, opening up to let my tongue lick along hers. She moans softly when my hand slides into her hair, gripping tightly.

I wonder what sounds she'd make as she came around my cock.

Fuck. No.

I need to stop thinking things like that. This thing between us has an expiration date. I like Bella, more than I should, but I'd be a fucking idiot to think the world's biggest pop star will want to explore anything with me after this. Right now, it makes sense. With any luck, we'll be the prince and princess of the Super Bowl. But then what? Once the stadium is empty and the confetti is swept away, I'll have nothing left to offer her. I'll start offseason training and she'll have the freedom she's been needing for the last ten years.

She pulls back, breathless from the kiss. "What was that for?" she asks, attempting to fix the lip gloss I just ruined.

"You were spiraling," I say with a shrug. I sit back in my seat but keep her hand in mine. "The more we touch and kiss in private, the more natural it'll look in public." I rub soothing circles on the top of her hand with my thumb. *I also just really love putting my tongue in your mouth.*

"Oh," she says quietly. "Yeah, that makes sense." Maybe I'm just delusional, but she almost looks disappointed with my explanation. I don't have time to read into that before the car comes to a stop in front of the restaurant's entrance. I look out the window to see several men and women holding cameras, waiting to get their shot. This is it, I guess.

Turning to Bella, I see some of the worry lingering from before. She's nothing like I thought she'd be. From the outside, she looks untouchable. Like she has all the confidence and gives zero fucks about what anyone thinks. But underneath all of that, she's just a regular girl who craves approval from the world. I want to be the one who tells her she's enough.

"Let's go over our game plan," I say confidently. "We'll get out and walk to the door. No hand holding yet. They know we're coming, so they already have a private table reserved for us where the cameras can't see. We'll eat our dinner, then walk back out, hand-in-hand. That's it. No big deal."

She relaxes before nodding her head. "Yeah. Okay. Let's do it."

I give her one more quick peck on the lips, just because, before opening the car door. I step out first, holding my hand out to help her out of the seat. As soon as she's standing, I drop her hand and shut the door. The flashes from the cameras almost blind me as we make our way toward the entrance. I know I'm supposed to keep my hands to myself until after dinner like Twyla said, but I can't help myself. Placing my hand on the small of her back, I lead Bella the rest of the way down the sidewalk and open the door, ushering her inside.

Fuck, that was intense. And we haven't even confirmed our relationship yet. I can't imagine the pandemonium once we do.

"Mr. Moran. Miss Simon," the hostess says as she grabs two menus and steps out from behind her desk. "Right this way."

This is a pretty high-class place, but that doesn't stop every patron in our path from gawking at Bella as we walk by. Just like Twyla said they would, some grab their phones and start typing away, no doubt alerting their friends and family of the fact that she's here with me. Not gonna lie...I feel like beating on my chest with my fists.

Bella Simon is *mine*. Even if it is all fake. They don't know that.

The hostess walks us behind a partition that divides our table from the rest of the place and motions for us to sit. I pull out Bella's chair, waiting for her to sit before I round the table and take my seat across from her. The hostess tells us our server will be right over before walking away. I immediately blow out a breath of relief. "Is it always like that?" I ask her.

She scoffs. "I wish. Twyla must've bribed the paps somehow for their silence. Normally, it's complete chaos once word gets out that I'm going somewhere. I usually end up having to leave before I'm ready because it's not safe."

I can't imagine dealing with that all the time. We deal with it to an extent, but it's not even a fraction of what Bella goes through. Blizzard fans have no problem coming up to me and asking for an autograph or photo, but they're cool with letting me go about my business once I give them what they want. I've never been forced to leave a place because of fans or cameras.

Just then, the server walks up beside us. "Hi. My name is Cassidy. I'll be your server for the evening. Can I start you off with—with some drinks?" she stutters. She's trying her best to keep her eyes from catching either of ours and I notice that she's holding her pad so tightly, her knuckles are white. This girl can't be more than seventeen.

"Hi, Cassidy," Bella says cheerfully. "I'm Bella. It's so nice to meet you." The girl looks up at her, cheeks pink with embarrassment as a wide smile blooms across her face. "This is a beautiful restaurant. Have you worked here long?"

"I started about a month ago," she says shyly. "My umm—my parents are the owners."

Bella gives the girl a soft smile. "That's really cool," she says. "I'd love a memory from tonight. Would you mind posing for a photo with me?" The girl goes completely white, like she just saw a ghost.

"You want a picture *with me*?" she asks, shocked.

"Yeah, if that's okay," Bella replies. "Mav, would you mind?" she says, handing me her phone.

I'm confused as fuck. But I take the phone from her extended hand as she stands up, putting her arm around the young girl. They both have big smiles on their faces as I snap the picture, handing Bella her phone back before we both take our seats. I stare in awe as she asks Cassidy for her Instagram, sends her a follow request, and DMs her the photo. The young server can barely contain herself.

"I should probably get your order in," she says. "I'm sure you want to get back to your date."

Bella looks at me. "Yeah, I do," she replies, never taking her eyes off mine. I almost believe her for a second, she's so convincing. I actually feel like she wants me with the way her heated stare is burning into my skin.

We give Cassidy our orders and she takes off, leaving us completely alone behind the partition. "What was the picture about?" I ask.

She smiles. *She's so fucking pretty.* "I could tell when she walked up that she was a fan. I knew she wouldn't ask for a photo, so I asked her for one instead. I just wanted to make her day."

"You're amazing, Bella. You know that?" It's my turn to stare. Only I think I actually *do* want her. Shit, this wasn't supposed to happen. I've only known Bella for less than a week and I'm already starting to feel things. Every day, I learn something else about her that I really like. But she's impossible to read. I'm not sure if this is starting to turn into something real for her or if she's just acting. I shouldn't be worried about any of this. Twyla asked me to do this and I should be sticking to the plan.

Forty-five minutes later, I've paid for our meal and left a large tip for Cassidy. Bella makes sure to sign an autograph, leaving it on the table before we make our way to the door. She pauses for a moment, exhaling slowly before turning to me. We're alone in the lobby, but the glass on the door is already showing me a preview of what awaits us outside. Paparazzi have lined the sidewalk along with at least fifty fans. It's a small area, so they're packed in tight next to one another as they wait for a glimpse of Bella Simon. Carlo, her driver and security guard, stands outside the door, ready to escort us to the car. I hate it. I want to be the one that protects her.

"Let's do this, Songbird," I say before grabbing her small hand in mine. I swing the door open, and all hell breaks loose. Cameras flash and fans start screaming as they all push their way toward us. Carlo has his arms wide, keeping them back so we can walk by. I've never seen anything like it in my life.

Suddenly, we're shoved from behind by the first row of people that were waiting for us as the ones behind them push forward to get a better view. Where I thought there were only fifty people, there were hundreds hiding off to the side. My only concern right now is getting Bella through this crowd safely. I pull her into my body, wrapping a protective arm around her as I push through. Fans are shouting at us so loudly; my ears are ringing by the time we make it to the car. Carlo has to push a few people back in order to open the door enough for me to help Bella inside, following her immediately.

As soon as the door closes, I have her face cradled in my hands, checking her for signs of distress. "Are you okay?"

"Yeah," she says, looking a bit shocked. I don't think she was expecting that mob of people any more than I was. "That was crazy."

"That's not normal, right?" I ask, relaxing into the seat now that I know she isn't hurt or upset.

She sighs. "Sometimes. But I usually have more security when it's a big group like that. I'm guessing my team didn't anticipate that many people rushing over here in such a short amount of time. I hope it isn't like that at the hotel."

She has a room booked for the evening so she can sleep before her jet takes her back to New York in the morning, but I don't like the idea of her going there alone. I know Carlo won't be far, but I still don't like it.

"Stay with me tonight," I say. "You can have the guest room again and you won't have to worry about anyone seeing you." I feel the desperation in my bones as I wait for her answer. I know I won't be able to sleep tonight unless I'm sure she's safe. And I can't be sure of that unless she's under the same roof as me.

She chews on her lip nervously. I want to reach out and pull it free from her teeth before soothing it with my tongue. But I don't. Instead, I wait for her to put me out of my misery.

"Okay," she says. "But under one condition."

"Anything," I reply, way quicker than I fucking should.

The corners of her plump lips turn up slightly. "Will you lay with me again?"

Fuck.

"Of course, I will, Songbird."

EIGHT
BELLA

CARLO PULLS into the underground parking lot and stops in front of the revolving door to let us out. I love that it's a private entrance and we don't have to worry about being bombarded by fans and paparazzi. As much as I love my fans, there are times where I just want a moment to myself. And even though I know the point of being with Mav is to be seen publicly, I find myself wanting to be alone with him. The way he held me tightly when we were making our way through the crowd back at the restaurant did something to me. I have five bodyguards and there have been times when all of them have surrounded me at once while I made my way through a sea of people, but I've never felt safer than I did with Maverick's arm possessively wrapped around me.

I know I shouldn't be agreeing to stay with him tonight. And I *definitely* shouldn't have requested that he lay in bed with me. But I want to be near him. I want his body pressed against mine again.

Over the past few days, I've been thinking a lot. We definitely crossed a line the first night on the couch. But I can't bring myself to really regret it. Coming on Maverick's lap was the most alive I've felt offstage in my whole life. I know this whole relationship is fake, but why can't I explore things with him physically while we're doing this? It's not like I can just run off and find someone else to do that with when I'm supposed to be dating Maverick. I'm twenty-four years old and I've only had sex once. Very unsatisfying sex, I might add. I want to know what it's like to feel pleasure until I can't take it anymore. So, why *can't* he be the guy that gives it to me? I can tell by the way he looks at me that there's chemistry. It may just be physical, but that's okay. He said he doesn't date during the season anyway, so casual sex is probably normal for him right now. As long as I can keep my feelings in check, we can totally make it work. Just because I want him to be the guy that shows me what sex should be like doesn't mean I need to fall in love with him. And I'm positive he won't be falling for me.

We make our way to the elevator, riding up to his floor. Nerves hit me out of nowhere when I think about everything I want. What if he says no? What if the kisses and touching really *were* just practice for the cameras? I have no idea how to seduce a guy. I don't even know where to start with trying to get him on board with fooling around some more.

Stop overthinking, Bella. Just see how it goes.

We sit in the living room, Schitt's Creek playing on the TV, while we wait for Carlo to bring my bags from the hotel. Thankfully, this time I was prepared for a night in Boston. All I can think about while we sit next to each other on the couch is the way he had me riding his lap right here the other night. How he gripped my hips and showed me the right angle to make myself feel good. How thick his cock felt rubbing against me.

I'm broken from my fantasy when his phone rings. "Hello," he says in greeting. "Yeah, I'll be right there." He stands. "Your bag is here. I'll grab it."

A minute later, he returns with my overnight bags in his hand. "Here you go," he says, handing them to me. "I'm going to jump in the shower. I'll use my ensuite. You can use the other bathroom." He smiles before taking off down the hall.

I go into the bathroom, throwing my hair up in a messy bun before I take a quick shower. After I'm dried off, I pull my silk pajama set out, mentally high-fiving myself for not bringing a ratty t-shirt and sweats to sleep in. I lotion my body, get dressed, and brush my teeth before returning to the living room. Maverick sits on the couch, engrossed in whatever is on his phone, wearing nothing but a pair of gray sweatpants. Good Lord, he's hot.

Catching his attention, he looks up at me. His mouth opens like he's going to say something, but he closes it, opting to take in my pajamas instead. I watch his Adam's apple bob as he swallows roughly. "Ready for bed?" he asks, his voice full of gravel.

"Yes," I reply. I'm internally freaking the fuck out, but I try to play it cool as I reach out my hand for him to take. He does, standing as I lead us to the guest room.

As I make my way down the hall, he pulls on my hand. "Do you want to sleep in my bed? It's more comfortable," he says.

Holy shit. This is really happening. I'm so nervous, I can feel my palm getting clammy in his.

"Umm, yeah," I whisper. I'm afraid if I talk louder, he'll hear my voice shaking. I haven't forgotten that this relationship is fake. But the way I want Maverick to touch me is very real. The anticipation of what actually might happen between us tonight has me ready to combust as I follow him into his room. It's all dark wood with a king-sized bed. The sheets and comforter are plush and white. They look like I could just sink into them, and they'd carry me off to dream land.

I try not to stare as Maverick pulls off his sweatpants, leaving him in only his black boxer briefs. He notices my avoidance and stops with them around his knees. "I, uhhh, normally sleep naked. Will it bother you if I'm in my underwear? I'll be too hot in these pants."

Too hot, indeed.

I shake my head frantically, trying not to look like an inexperienced almost-virgin. "No! You're fine," I say, entirely too enthusiastically. I'm awkward enough with guys as it is, but this *particular* guy, in only his underwear, is making my brain short circuit. He removes his pants, throwing them over a chair in the corner before he pulls back the covers. I slide into bed next to him and lay on my back, pulling the duvet up to my neck.

It's official. I don't know what I'm doing.

I read romance books all the time with strong female characters who see a man they want and seduce him into doing filthy things to them. They make it seem so easy, but here I am, stiff as a board, not knowing what I should do next to let Maverick know that I want him to put his hands on me.

When I finally get the courage to look over at him, I see the same expression on his face. He can't be nervous, right? His body language speaks to the contrary. His muscles are tense, fists balled tight. The duvet is pulled over his bottom half, and I can see the rapid rise and fall of his chest as he breathes.

It's now or never. If I want this to go anywhere, I need to make a move.

"Maverick?" I whisper into the dark room. The only light is coming from the full moon outside, but it illuminates enough that I can see his eyes as we turn toward each other.

"Yeah?" he says.

I slowly exhale, building up the courage to ask for what I want. "Do you think we could, um, practice some more?"

His eyes are hooded as he reaches out and grabs ahold of my hand. "I'm afraid I'm going to need you to be more specific, Songbird. What exactly do you want from me? I need you to say it."

Fuck. Why is he doing this to me? My biggest fear is asking for something from someone who doesn't want to give it. That's why I'm just happy doing what I'm told and never voicing my own wishes. It's better than feeling like I'm burdening people because they don't want to tell me no.

Sensing my uneasiness, he lets go of my hand, bringing one of his to my face.

"Bella, I have a feeling you'd rather do almost anything than tell someone out loud what you want. Just so you know, I'll give it all to you. Anything you ask for; it's yours. I just need you to tell me." He waits for a moment, and when I don't answer right away, he speaks again. "You deserve it. And I want to be the lucky one that you trust enough to ask," he whispers before pressing a soft kiss to my lips.

I exhale a shaky breath. "I want everything," I say. "I

want your hands and mouth on my body, Maverick. *Please.*" I beg.

"That's my girl. I'm so proud of you for telling me what you need," he praises, and it makes my muscles clench down low. He starts by kissing me again, but this time it feels different. It's like he's finally allowing himself to let loose. He moves his lips down my face, trailing wet kisses over my throat as his hands begin to explore my body. He sucks on the sensitive skin of my neck, hands tracing the hem of my camisole before moving underneath the thin fabric. I moan loudly when his fingertips graze my nipple. My whole body is on high alert. I can already feel my orgasm starting to bloom to life and he hasn't even really touched me yet.

When I bring my legs together, squeezing my thighs tightly to relieve the ache that's made itself very apparent, he pulls his mouth from mine. "You need some help?" he coos. "You asked so nicely for my hands and mouth. Let me take care of you." He gets up on his knees beside me, reaching for my sleep shorts and sliding them down my legs. He presses his forehead to mine as he slowly lowers his hand down my body, stopping at my mound that's still covered by the thin lace panties I'm wearing. I gasp when he uses his middle finger to apply pressure to my opening, just barely pushing my panties inside me. "Does that feel good?" he asks. All I can do is nod my head as I take rapid, shallow breaths.

"Mav," I manage to choke out when he moves the pressure to my clit, rubbing in tight circles over my underwear. I feel like I could come apart right now, just like this. I allow my body to do what it wants, my hips thrusting into his hand with every stroke.

"That's it, pretty girl. Take your pleasure," he whispers,

not stopping or slowing down as I continue chasing my release. I've never wanted anything so bad. When he pulls his head back, looking down at where his hand is working me, I see the determination on his face. He wasn't lying. He wants to take care of me. The thought brings me even closer to the edge as my pussy begins trying to tighten around the emptiness inside me.

"Fuck. Maverick. I— I can't," I whine. I'm right there, but the contact just isn't enough to send me over the edge.

"I've got you, baby," he says, sliding his hand under the waistband of my panties. As soon as I feel the pressure of his finger entering me, I'm there.

"Oh my God, please don't stop," I whimper.

"I'm not going to stop. I promise," he says. "Just be my perfect girl and come for me."

The praise does the trick. I come so hard as he gently thrusts his finger in and out. My body shakes violently as I dig my fingernails into his firm bicep, holding him to me.

When it becomes too sensitive, I let go of his arm and he decreases the pressure, lightly stroking the rim of my pussy. I don't know if it's possible, but I already feel like I need another orgasm. I pull on the back of his neck, kissing him frantically as I lift my hips from the bed.

"You're a greedy little thing, aren't you?" he asks. I tense slightly, wondering if he wants to stop. Or if he wants me to do something for him.

As if he has a direct line to my brain, he stops, looking straight into my eyes. "Bella, I'm just teasing you. There's absolutely nowhere else I want to be than right here with you, taking care of your needs. If that changes, I'll let you know. Okay?"

God damn my fake boyfriend for being so perfect. He's

making it really hard not to feel like I want more from him than just this.

I nod my head. "Yeah. Okay," I whisper.

"Good," he says with a smirk. "Because I might die if I don't get to taste you."

MAVERICK

I can't even see straight with the need to put my tongue on this woman. My cock is heavy in my boxer briefs, smearing pre-cum all over the inside of the material. She didn't ask me to fuck her yet, but she might. And just from putting one finger inside her, I know I'll hurt her if I don't get her really ready. She has the tightest pussy I've ever felt. If she hadn't told me herself, I would definitely think she was a virgin.

I kiss my way down her stomach, licking and teasing at her soft skin. I slowly peel her panties down her legs before throwing them to the floor. I can see how wet she is. Her body shivers as I settle my shoulders between her legs. Just as I go to put my mouth on her, she pushes me back.

"Wait," she says frantically, sitting up. I immediately back up, thinking she's pulling the plug. If she wants it to stop, it stops. But, fuck, I need to know what I did wrong. "I, um—," she says, avoiding eye contact with me. "I've never done this before."

Fuuuuck me.

My cock that was already harder than it's ever been, turns to stone as I think about the fact that her cunt has never been tasted by anyone. I'll be her first. I have to make this perfect for her.

I do my best to soften my expression. I know she's

embarrassed by her inexperience. "That's so fucking hot, baby," I rasp. "I'm honored that you're giving this to me. If you still want to, I mean."

She exhales before leaning back onto her elbows and spreading her legs further for me before she nods her head slowly. That's all the affirmation I need as I lean forward and softly press my lips to her swollen clit. She jumps at the contact, so I back off, gently massaging her inner thighs with my thumbs. "I promise, I'll make you feel so good, Songbird. Just be a good girl and relax for me," I say as I poke out my tongue, tracing the outside of her lips. Her low moan tells me that she likes that move, so I repeat it.

Now that she's finally relaxed, I use my thumb and pointer finger to spread the delicate skin covering her clit, latching my lips around it and sucking.

"Fuck!" she curses. And it's like a jolt straight to my dick. I want to make her say the dirtiest things. Alternating from sucking to licking, I bring her close to the edge, but slow down before she's able to orgasm. I need her as wet as possible.

I use the pointer finger on my other hand and push it into her, satisfied at how easily I'm sliding in now. She's still tight as fuck, but I think I'll be able to fit. I pick up the pace, fingering and licking her in earnest as I feel her begin to clench around me.

"Mav," she whines.

"I know. I know, baby. You need to come so bad, don't you?" I coo. "Go ahead and do it. Come in my mouth. I'm fucking desperate for it."

I know I shouldn't because it's probably going to scare the fuck out of her, but I can't help myself. I curl my finger forward, finding her g-spot with ease. Just as I pull her clit back between my lips, I use my free hand to put pressure on her lower abdomen.

"Oh my God, Maverick, wait!" she screams, trying to pull her body away from me, but I hold her in place. A moment later, her pussy strangles my finger as she soaks my mouth and chin. Her body convulses wildly as I swallow every drop I can catch, flattening my tongue and licking her clean as her orgasm subsides.

Then, I brace myself for her reaction.

She looks down at me, horrified at her arousal that's still dripping down my chin. "Is that—?"

"No!" I say hurriedly. "It's cum. You squirted for me," I tell her. I know she's probably mortified, which she definitely shouldn't be, but I want her to be comfortable with all of the things I do to her.

"Oh, my Goddddddd," she groans into her hands, which are now covering her face. "I'm so sorry."

I chuckle, placing one last kiss to her sensitive core before I make my way back up her body. Pulling her hands from her face, I give her a playful smirk. "Don't apologize for that. I fucking loved it," I assure her.

She furrows her brows. "You— really?"

"Yes, Songbird. I'm so fucking hard right now." I punctuate the sentiment by thrusting my covered cock into her leg so she can feel for herself what she does to me. Even doing that feels like heaven. "I want you," I whisper. I didn't even mean to say it. Normally, I'm in control in these situations, but with Bella, I feel desperate for her.

"Then have me," she replies, kissing my neck. I can't help the low groan that leaves me at the contact.

I reluctantly put some space between us, leaning back so I can look at her. "Are you sure?" I ask. "We don't have to do anything. I want you to do things for *you*."

She swallows nervously. "I can't remember ever wanting anything the way I want you right now, Maverick. Please don't make me beg."

The thought of her on her knees, begging for my cock makes me almost come on the spot. But I've pushed her out of her comfort zone a lot already tonight, so we'll save that for another time. I reach over to my nightstand and pause abruptly. "Fuck, baby. We can't," I say, disappointment dripping from my tone. "I don't have any condoms. I never fuck during the season."

She lets out a slow breath. "I have an IUD. I got it before—" she pauses, which I'm glad for because I definitely don't want to hear about her with another man. "I've had it for a couple of years. And I'm clean. I haven't been with anyone since my first time."

I sigh in relief. "I got tested before the season started. I'm good."

"Okay," she whispers, reaching down and palming my cock. "I want you to fuck me, Maverick."

Holy fuck. There's nothing hotter than Bella asking for what she wants. I pull her pajama top over her head, leaving her completely naked. Her tits are small and perky. I can't wait to see how sensitive they really are when I take them into my mouth as I fuck her.

I reach down, shucking my boxer briefs before settling back down on top of her. I kiss her as I rub my length up and down her wet slit. She stills, pulling back and looking between us. "Is that going to fit?" she asks, a look of fear melting over her features.

"That's why I made you squirt, baby," I say, hoping it reassures her a little bit. "You're really wet, and we'll go slow. I won't hurt you."

She nods her head and I feel her legs relax, letting me

settle in closer. I distract her with another kiss as I gently push the crown of my cock inside her. She gasps, eyes slamming shut tight. I stop, staying still so she can adjust. This is going to take all my self-control, but I'd cut my dick off before I'd ever hurt her.

"You're doing so good," I praise. "Your pussy feels amazing." I feel her relax slightly at my words, letting me push another inch inside. Pulling back so I'm barely sheathed by her, I thrust forward gently until I meet resistance. Bella moans, so I go a little deeper. She's got me in a fucking vice grip, getting wetter with every movement of my hips.

When I don't feel like I can go any further without hurting her, I reach between us, rubbing her swollen clit with my thumb. Her inner walls slowly relax more, letting me slide the rest of my length into her. "Good fucking girl, Bella. Look at how beautiful your cunt is, taking my big cock."

"Mav, I'm so full," she says in astonishment as she raises her head to look at where we're joined.

"Keep watching, baby," I tell her. "Watch me move in and out of you." I know this is all new for her, but I can tell that she likes the dirty talk. I can *feel* what it's doing to her.

I start slowly, dragging my cock out to the head, then pushing back inside. "That's it, beautiful. Thank you for keeping me nice and wet so I can fuck you. You're doing such a good job for me." She moans at the praise, loosening enough so I can thrust into her harder. She's still watching my cock go in and out, but I can't take my eyes off her face. She's flushed and sweaty, pieces of her golden hair sticking to her smooth skin.

Fuck. I'm a goner.

When Twyla told me I'd be Bella Simon's fake boyfriend, I was intrigued. But I also thought she'd be different than she is. Where I expected a stuck up, bossy princess who got everything she asked for handed to her on a silver platter, she's anything but. She's kind, giving, and probably the most selfless person I've ever met. The few times I've made her ask me for what she wants, she struggled because she's not used to it. I want to change that more than anything.

I lean down, kissing her passionately as I gently fuck her. Everything about this moment feels monumental. Like a shift is happening between us as she hands me the keys to her pleasure. All I can think about is never giving them back. Being the man she comes to when she wants to feel good.

That thought brings me back to the present just as Bella's legs begin to shake around my hips. I grab under her knee, spreading her more as I pick up my pace. The change in position has her walls fluttering as she starts to milk me. "There you go. Come all over me," I growl.

"Oh, fuck," she whimpers. "Mav. I'm gonna—" Her words are choked off as her orgasm crashes over her. Her tight pussy grips me so hard, black dances around the edges of my vision. The pressure on my cock is borderline painful as she rides out her release, but I keep a steady tempo for her.

When I'm sure she's completely spent, I slow just enough to not overstimulate her. I know she's sensitive, but it doesn't take long before my balls begin to draw up, the tightness tingling all over my body as she whimpers under me. "Baby, where do you want me to come?" I ask. She said she has an IUD, but that doesn't mean she doesn't want me to pull out.

"Come inside me," she whispers. "I want all of you. I *need* all of you."

Her desperate words push me over as I bust inside her. It's the hardest I've ever come in my life. It just keeps going as I feel my seed dripping out of her while I continue thrusting wildly. The obscene sound it makes fills the room as I finally begin to slow my movements, lowering my forehead to hers. We both sit there, still joined, as we attempt to catch our breath.

"That was amazing," I whisper. "*You* are amazing." I press a soft kiss to her lips, pushing a rogue strand of hair behind her ear. "Are you okay?"

"Mmhmm," she hums contentedly.

I chuckle before reluctantly pulling out. I watch as my cum leaks out of her, sliding down her ass crack and pooling on the bed beneath her. Before I can stop myself, I scoop up a drop that's trying to escape, pushing it back into her. She whimpers, making me realize how red and swollen she is. "Does it hurt?" I ask, worried.

"It's a little sore," she says. "And really sensitive."

I drop a gentle kiss to her stomach before I get up from the bed. "I'll be right back," I tell her. "Don't move."

She laughs softly, "Couldn't even if I wanted to."

I walk into the bathroom, turning the tap to fill up the giant custom bathtub. I root around under the cupboard until I find some aromatherapy bubble bath and pour in a small amount. Returning to the bedroom, I scoop up a very tired Bella and carry her, bridal style, back into the ensuite before stepping into the hot water. She barely stirs as I lower us down beneath the suds. If it weren't for her snuggling her face into my neck, I'd assume she was asleep.

We sit there, clinging to one another until the water

turns cold. I wish we could stay here forever, never having to worry about going back to our fake relationship or being in the public eye. I'd be lying if I said this thing doesn't suddenly feel like a lot more than just a PR stunt. But I have no idea if Bella is on the same page. We both have busy lives, and our main focus will always be our careers, so I can't imagine she'd want to make this work between us. Plus, she's so close to getting the first real break she's had in a decade, so it would be selfish of me to ask her for that time she worked so hard to earn. I need to stick to the original plan. We keep this thing strictly business, perform for the cameras, and break up amicably after the Super Bowl. Then, she's free to do whatever she wants while I start training for next season.

Until then, it won't hurt to pretend she really is mine.

NINE

MAVERICK

I WALK THROUGH THE CORRIDOR, cameras flashing everywhere as I make my way toward the locker room. We play Tennessee today, and a win can clinch us a spot in the playoffs. Normally, I'm in the zone this close to game time, but all I can think about is the fact that Bella will be here today. It is, as Twyla called it, our *hard launch*. Even though we were photographed leaving Donatello's earlier this week, we haven't actually confirmed that we're dating. We'll be going fully public with our fake relationship today and I have to admit that my head is all over the place about it. I'm still aware that it isn't real, but after the night we shared, I'm having trouble not feeling things for Bella.

"Maverick!" one of the reporters yells. "Rumor has it that Bella Simon will be at the game today. Can you confirm or deny that?"

Sticking to the plan we went over this morning, I give a charming wink, but say nothing as I walk through the doors into the locker room. Immediately, I can feel the somber ambiance around me as I step up to my locker, setting my bag inside. I look around, finding Blaze Beckham sitting on a bench, bent over with his head in his hands. Dalton Davis stands at his side, quietly speaking as our quarterback, Tanner Lake, nods his head in agreement.

I tip my chin to one of our other receivers, Landyn Riley. "What's going on over there?" I ask.

"I'm not really sure," he says quietly. "Becks came in, punched the wall by his locker, and Davis and Lake have been trying to calm him down ever since."

Fuck. I hope he's okay. Blaze is a really good guy and he's pretty much always happy. I hate to see him upset like this. Even though we don't know every detail about each other's personal lives, this team is a family. When one of us is going through a rough time, we're all going through it together.

I try to focus on getting my head right, trusting that Dalton and Tanner have things under control as they talk to Blaze. I put in my AirPods with intentions of firing up my pre-game hype playlist, but I find myself pulling up Bella's latest album on Spotify. As soon as her voice hits my ears, my whole body calms. She's so fucking good. I hum along to her newest single, *Glass Hearts,* nodding my head along to the beat. I just saw her two days ago, and we've been texting non-stop, but I miss her. All I've been thinking about is being able to kiss her wherever I want, no matter who's watching.

I just need to go out there and get this win in the bag so I can claim her in front of the whole world.

BELLA

"This is insane!" I say to Twyla as we watch the Blizzard defense run out onto the field. The fans are screaming at the top of their lungs, hoping the guys can make a stop here in order to win the game. My dad and brother are huge football fans, so I understand the rules enough to make sense of things. Although, I made a list in my notes app to ask Maverick later on. Honestly, why do they run it up the middle so much when it hardly ever works? And why does the term 'strip sack' sound so dirty?

The crowd gets even louder, booing the refs as they call a complete pass when the receiver's foot was definitely out of bounds. "Booooooo!" I yell with my hands cupped around my mouth. It's just Twyla and me in the suite, and the glass windows make it impossible to hear me, but I don't care. Mav knows where I am.

Thankfully, the call is overturned, giving the defense another chance to make the stop. It's fourth down and there are fifteen seconds left in the game. Tennessee needs eight yards for a first down. The ball is snapped, and Maverick moves quickly, rolling off the blocker. Nothing stands between him and the quarterback, who never sees him coming as he makes the sack. I go nuts, jumping up and down while screaming into the empty room. I'm so proud of him.

Mav pops up, looks directly at me, and points. *Well, these panties are going in the trash.* Just as Twyla planned, the cameras pan to me, broadcasting my face on the Jumbotron and probably televisions across the country. Looking down at him, I wave before blowing him a kiss.

"That was perfect," Twyla says quietly as the offense takes the field, kneeling to run the final seconds off the clock. She turns to me. "So, we have a small change of plans." I listen intently as she continues. "We weren't expecting the fans to be so interested in you making an appearance here today, but they are. Some managed to slip past security earlier. We got them out, but we feel that it's unsafe to have you moving around the stadium right now. Maverick is going to go do his post-game stuff, take a shower, and then he'll come up here. Meanwhile, I'll get a few reporters that I trust to take photos of the two of you leaving."

It's always scary when people get past security, but it's not nearly as uncommon as I wish it was. I'm sure Carlo and his team are refusing to put me in danger, so we'll have to make things work up here.

"Okay," I tell her.

She gives me a thumbs up. "I'm going to go wrangle some paps. I don't know how long it'll take me, so make yourself comfortable in here. Maverick and I are the only ones who are allowed past security, so you won't have to worry about anybody else getting in here. I'll be back as soon as I can."

When she leaves, I hear the click of the lock engaging before I walk back over to the window. Blizzard fans are mostly filing out toward the exit, and I see some of the maintenance staff beginning to clean up. Looking at the field, I visualize my halftime performance stage. The game isn't here in Boston, but I'm sure the field in L.A. isn't much different. I imagine myself running out while the fans scream for me as I sing my opening number. My dancers and I hit every step of our choreography perfectly. I think of Maverick, who will hopefully be playing in the game, wishing he could be watching me as his coach gives a compelling halftime speech. I feed off the energy of the crowd while I sing my heart out because it's what I love.

I'm pulled from my daydream when I hear a soft beep, followed by the lock on the door clicking. I guess Twyla works quick.

I'm surprised when it's Maverick that walks into the room. He looks absolutely delicious in his grey sweatpants and Blizzard hoodie. His hair is wet, likely from his post-game shower. "What are you doing here? I thought you had to—"

I'm cut off by him rushing my way in three long strides and pressing his lips roughly to mine. I melt into him as he brings his hands to my cheeks, tilting my head so he can deepen the kiss. Our tongues battle one another as he swallows each and every one of my moans. Honestly, I'm pretty sure the only reason I haven't fallen to the floor like a boneless pile of mush is because he has such a tight hold on my face.

Holy shit.

We kiss like that for several minutes before he finally pulls away. I miss his lips immediately.

"What was that for?" I ask, still breathless.

He slides his hands down my body, stopping to gently hold onto my waist. "I'm not sure," he says on a laugh. "Just felt like I needed it."

I allow myself to stay in the moment with him. Right now, I'm not thinking about this being fake. Or if people will believe us. Or what the media will say. My only concern is how good it feels to be his. Even if it does have an expiration date.

The door opens and Twyla steps in. Maverick doesn't make an effort to move away, so I lean to the side to see past his massive frame.

"Well, don't you two just look like the perfect couple?" she says, excitedly. "I love the commitment, but you guys don't have to put on an act unless the cameras are around."

Realization rears its ugly head. I know what we signed

up for, but I miss being in Mav's apartment, where we can just be ourselves and not have to worry about who's watching.

She must notice the change in my demeanor because she gives us a stern look before she speaks again. "You two are still good with this plan, right?" she asks. "You need to be one hundred percent on board for everything, from the public appearances to the staged break-up. If the fans find out what we're pulling here, our careers will be ruined."

I go to open my mouth, but I'm cut off when Maverick speaks. "We understand. It's strictly business. We're sticking to the plan." I look up to find his expression completely void of any emotion. Like he didn't just kiss me completely breathless five minutes ago because he '*just needed it*'. I can't lie. It hurts.

Shit. I'm getting emotionally attached. No matter how many times I tell myself this is fake, I can't help it. Even hearing him confirm it, I still find it hard to believe the things we've shared so far have meant nothing to him. Then again, he probably treats all the girls he sleeps with like they're special.

I swallow roughly as I nod my head in agreement. I don't trust my voice not to betray me if I speak. Pushing down the feelings of rejection, I put on the mask of confidence I always use when I want people to think my life is perfect while I wait for her to tell us what kind of performance we'll be putting on for the cameras when we walk out this door.

"Okay, great!" she says with a clap. "I have about ten photographers and reporters standing at the end of the hall. Just go out there and show them how smitten you are. Do it however you want, but I need you to really sell it. These are the pictures that people will be talking about for months!"

Maverick grabs my hand and I go still, but recover quickly. Giving him the realest looking fake smile I can manage, we head out the door and down the hall, where the media waits for us. As soon as we come into view, camera shutters fill my ears while flashes go off in every direction. I look up at Maverick, who is staring down at me with a genuine smile on his face. *Damn, he's good at this.* Before I can work through the mixed signals he's giving, he turns, wrapping his arms around me before lifting me off the ground. When his lips touch mine briefly, I try to forget his coldness as he told Twyla we were keeping things strictly business. Thankfully, I think everyone around us buys it. He sets me back down, nuzzling my nose with his before pulling me into the open elevator.

The doors close, leaving us alone in the quiet space. I don't say anything. I can't. I knew exactly what was being asked of me when I agreed to this fake relationship. I can't be mad at him for not diverting from the plan just because I asked him to have sex with me. Maverick is a great guy and I know he would never intentionally hurt me.

But I guess I'm pretty stellar at hurting myself.

The elevator dings and the doors open to reveal the team parking garage. I pull my hand from his now that I know we aren't in the public eye and follow him to his car. I don't wait for him to open my door before sliding inside and buckling up without a word while he throws his bag in the trunk. *Real mature, Bella.*

He settles into the driver's seat, gripping the wheel, but not turning the key. "What's wrong?" he asks.

"Nothing. I'm fine," I reply. I don't even bother to pretend to smile. "I'm just tired."

"Okay," he says on a forced exhale as he starts the car and heads toward his building. The plan was for me to stay with him again because Carlo really likes the security situation there. I have to agree, especially now that the fans know I'm in the city. They're very determined when they want to find out what hotel I'm staying at. But right now, I feel like I'd rather walk back to New York than be stuck in the same apartment with Maverick while I try to process my feelings.

Thankfully, traffic isn't too bad, and we make it to his place quicker than I expected. I'm glad he had the radio on the whole way because I honestly wouldn't have known what to say to him. At least not until I get my emotions in check. Which I definitely need to do if we're going to make it to Super Bowl as a believable couple.

Maverick pulls up to the valet and I swing the door open again before he can make his way around the car. I wait by the revolving door as he grabs both of our bags from the trunk. I walk ahead of him to the elevator and I'm relieved to see the attendant sitting on a stool inside, because that means Mav won't try asking me what's wrong again. What am I supposed to say? *"I think I might be falling in love with you even though none of this was ever supposed to be real."*

Absolutely fucking not.

The door opens into Maverick's apartment, and I take my bag from his hand. "Thank you," I say quietly. "I'm, umm, really tired. Goodnight." Before he can reply, I hightail it to the guest room, shutting the door behind me. I look at my watch, giving myself exactly two minutes to let my emotions out. Flopping face first onto the bed, I let tears of frustration fall onto the comforter. I even allow my intrusive thoughts to scream at me, telling me why this will never be more than a PR stunt.

"He can do better."

"You're too inexperienced."

"He'll never love you back."

When my time is up, I dry my eyes and look into the mirror. My makeup is smeared, and my eyes are red. I look exactly how I feel. I pause, listening for Maverick moving around, but I'm met with complete silence. Hoping he went to bed, I ease the door open and see total darkness, save for the nightlight he has in the hallway. I turn back into the room and grab my overnight bag before quietly darting into the hall. I need a shower, so hopefully I can make it to the bathroom without being seen. As I pass his bedroom door, it swings open. A shirtless Maverick steps out, blocking the path to my destination.

"Excuse me," I say faintly.

"Not until you tell me why you aren't in my bed," he replies.

I try to slide past him, but he moves with me. "Bella, what did I do? You haven't said two words to me since we left the suite."

I avoid looking at his face because I know if I do, I'll start crying again. That *can't* happen. If he finds out that I'm emotionally attached, it could ruin everything. "I told you. I'm tired," I lie.

"Bullshit," he says. "We might not have known each other that long, but I can tell you're upset. Talk to me, baby. Please," he pleads.

I try to move past him again, to no avail. "*Don't* call me that," I spit. "I'm not your baby. This is strictly business, remember?" Fuck. I didn't want to show my cards like this. I didn't want him to know how deeply his words back at the stadium cut me. Now I'm acting like a clingy girlfriend. I'm sure the last thing he wants is this kind of drama. He avoids relationships during the season for that very reason.

"Bella, I didn't mean—"

"No," I cut him off. "You're right. This isn't real. I don't expect you to placate me just because I got my feelings hurt a little. It was my fault anyway. I got confused by all the kissing. And the sex. We shouldn't have done that. I don't think I know how to do casual."

God, I sound pathetic.

He stands there silently for a moment while I continue looking at everything but him. I'm hoping he will just let it go. Let me by him so I can take a shower, go back to the guest room, and sleep until it's time to catch my plane back to New York. But he doesn't. Instead, he grabs me by the hips and walks me backward until I'm pushed up against the wall.

"Baby," he says, emphasizing the word. "I only said that because we got caught kissing and Twyla seemed to be spiraling. I know how much trouble we could all be in if people found out that we agreed to be in a fake relationship, so I was easing her mind. I like you. I don't know what any of this means for us, but we have until Super Bowl to figure it out. I don't want to spend all that time with you being upset at me." He nuzzles his face into my neck, inhaling. "I can't sleep knowing you're down the hall. I need you in bed with me."

He gently presses his lips to my sensitive skin, making me shiver. My resolve is hanging by a thread as he pulls back and gives me a soft smile. "I'm sorry," he whispers.

Damn him for being so sweet. Maybe I'm a weak bitch, or maybe I do just want to enjoy the time we have. We'll figure out the rest later. "Don't be," I tell him. "I over-reacted."

"No," he says sternly. "Don't do that. I fucked up. I shouldn't have said those things to Twyla. I didn't mean them. And they hurt you. I owe you an apology."

Nobody has ever cared about my feelings the way Maverick does. I mean, don't get me wrong. My parents were very nurturing when I was growing up. But it's been so long since they've really been around me on a day-to-day basis. I deal with a lot of people who tell me what to do and when to do it. None of them ever ask if I'm happy. And when I'm not, they certainly don't try to spare my feelings or apologize. To be honest, I can't remember the last time anyone told me they were sorry. I'm always the one saying it. But with Maverick, I know he's sincere. And maybe the bar is just really low, but it means the world to me that he's owning the fact that he hurt me.

"I forgive you," I say, trying to hold back my tears.

He exhales a breath of relief before leaning down to kiss me. "Next time I upset you, and there will be a next time because I'm new at this, don't shut me out. I will never hurt you on purpose, okay?" He uses his thumb to wipe away the single tear that escaped, despite my efforts. I don't know why I'm so emotional over his apology, but I can't speak without my voice wobbling, so I just nod my head in understanding.

"That's my girl," he says. "Now, go take a shower and get that sweet ass in my bed where you belong."

TEN
MAVERICK

I WAKE SLOWLY, Bella's small moans registering in my ears as I feel her lips roam my naked body. I could definitely get used to mornings like this. Last night after her shower, she walked into my room wearing nothing but a towel and I fucked her until I was sure she accepted my apology. We fell asleep, completely exhausted, wrapped up in one another.

I focus on my girl as she kisses her way down my torso, her tongue dragging along the defined lines of my abs. I gently run my hands through her hair as my breathing gets heavier.

"Are you awake?" she whispers.

I chuckle quietly, my voice full of sleep. "Kinda hard not to be when your mouth is all over me. I didn't want to miss it."

She hums as she makes her way even lower, licking the sensitive skin above my dick. "Can you tell me how to do it?"

Fuck. Me.

Sometimes I forget that there are things Bella has never

done. I know she's embarrassed by it, but I meant it when I told her it was hot. The fact that she trusts me enough to give me so many of her firsts makes me almost feral. I want to give her everything she wants. I want to take care of her body.

I shove my pillow further under my head so I can see her better. "Use your tongue. Tease me with it," I say. She obeys, running her hot, wet tongue up the length of my shaft. She takes her time, treating me like the most delicious lollipop she's ever tasted. I look down, thankful for the morning light that's filtering through the curtains. She looks like an angel, her long, silky hair framing her face as she worships my cock.

When I can't take it any longer, I give her more instruction. "That feels so fucking good, Songbird. Now take me into your mouth." Using her hand, she grips the base of my dick, holding it straight up as she lowers her mouth over my tip and sucks. I'm seeing stars already, my restraint beginning to break. I need to keep myself calm while she does this. As much as I want to take her hair in my fists and fuck her face, she needs to explore.

My toes curl when she begins working my thickness into her mouth. I'm big, and most of the girls I've been with have given up once they realized it takes work to take all of me in their mouths, but not Bella. The determination in her expression is making me feel like I could blow right now as she struggles to stretch her lips around me.

"Fuck, baby," I choke out. "You don't have to go any further." But she doesn't pull back. In fact, she doubles down, continuing to work me toward the back of her throat. I can't help the involuntary jerk of my hips that makes her gag. "I'm so sorry," I say. "Are you okay?"

"Do it again," she whispers.

Fuck. Sounds like maybe my girl has a dirty side neither of us knows about. I decide to test the waters. "You like gagging on my cock, Bella? You want me to fuck your beautiful face?"

"Mhmmm," she hums, lowering her mouth back onto me.

I am painfully hard thinking about it, but I need to let her adjust to me first. I tighten my hand in her hair slightly, making her wince before her expression relaxes again. "Work me to the back of your throat for a bit. Then when you're nice and stretched out for me, I'll take over." Like the good girl she is, Bella continues moving her perfect mouth up and down, her jaw muscles relaxing more and more every second. When I feel like she's ready, I pull her off me with a pop. "Get on your knees on the floor for me, baby," I order.

She moves to stand, and I follow her before she slowly sinks down. "Good fucking girl, Bella," I praise. "Look at you, so eager to swallow my cock." Her eyes widen with anticipation as she waits for me to tell her what to do. "I'm going to fuck your face. If it's too much or you just want me to stop, tap twice on my thigh. You're still in control here," I remind her. I want her to know that just because she's giving me this, it doesn't mean we can't pull the plug at any time if she wants to.

"Okay," she whispers, looking up at me like I'm her god.

"Open that pretty mouth for me, baby," I order. She does, inviting me to push past her plump lips. I start slowly, making small, lazy movements as she gets used to the sensations. When I feel her jaw relax, I weave my hands into her hair and thrust harder. I push back as far as I can, making her gag, but she takes it like a champ. When

I look down at her, I feel my balls pull up tight, tingling as my release starts to build. She's looking up at me, eyes full of unshed tears from gagging, as I pump myself over and over into her heavenly mouth. She has her mouth open as far as it will go, letting me use her however I want. Drool spills over her lips, coating my cock and running down her chin.

"Fuck. You're doing such a good job, Bella. You're going to make me come. Do you want to taste it? Or do you want me to cover that pretty face of yours?"

She pulls off me, panting. "Both."

That one word is all it takes for my orgasm to barrel through me. I grip my dick and jerk furiously until the hot liquid shoots into her open mouth. I angle upward slightly, hitting her face with more ropes of cum until I'm completely spent. She closes her mouth, swallowing before dragging her tongue across her bottom lip.

"You are a fucking goddess, baby," I say on an exhale before hauling her to her feet and crushing my lips to hers. I don't give a single fuck that she's covered in my release. I just need to be close to her. I turn us, tossing her on the bed as she squeals with laughter. Just as I go to bury my face between her legs, my phone rings, the sound popping our little bubble. I reach over, icing the call, but seconds later, Bella's rings.

She lets out a frustrated huff before crawling up to the nightstand. "It's Twyla," she says nervously.

"It's fine. Act natural. She doesn't have to know your face is covered in me." I wink, earning the cutest little eye roll as she answers her phone.

"Hello?" she says as I run to the en-suite to grab a warm washcloth for her face. I laugh to myself as I notice the rasp in her voice from the way she was just gagging on me. Making a mental note to make her some tea this morning, I hold the cloth under the tap, soaking it completely. I return to the bed, reluctantly wiping the remnants of my orgasm off Bella's cheeks as she continues the conversation.

"Wow," she says, her eyebrows shooting up. "That's insane."

I catch her eyes, furrowing my brows in confusion, but she puts up one finger, as if telling me to "hold on".

She continues. "Well, that's what we wanted, right?" I take a seat next to her on the bed, grabbing her by the waist and sliding her toward me because I apparently need to cling to her at all times now. She leans her head into my chest as I run my fingers through her hair.

"Yeah, I'm still at his apartment. I'll let him know. And you can text me the details." She sits up. "Okay, bye," she says before hitting the end button and tossing the phone on the bed.

"Well, everyone is going nuts over the photos from last night," she tells me. "Rumor has it we've been sneaking around for months and we're already planning to move in together." She smirks.

I know how fast word can spread, even when it's made up. Normally, I get annoyed by it. But for some reason, that particular rumor makes me feel warm and excited. I know this started out fake, but the feelings I'm developing for Bella are very real to me. And thinking of a future where I am waking up beside her every day doesn't sound bad at all.

I pull her along the bed until we're both settled back under the covers. "Well, we should definitely practice that by staying in my bed all day long," I tell her, dropping my lips to her neck. I have the day off today and she doesn't have rehearsal for the halftime performance until this evening.

"I wish," she groans. "Twyla wants us to go out today. She set up for some photographers to follow us while we go—" she pauses, a look of worry clouding her features.

"Go what?" I ask.

"She wants us to get a Christmas tree."

"Okayyyyyyyy," I say, drawing out the word. "What's wrong with that?" I ask.

She shrugs. "That's a pretty big tradition for most people. I don't want to intrude on that by being some outsider hanging around while you decorate."

I kiss her lips gently. "Baby, you're not an outsider. And I would love to go get a tree with you," I reassure her. "Honestly, I wasn't planning on getting one at all because I didn't feel like I needed it. I usually go home for Christmas, but we play that day, so I won't be able to." My heart squeezes in my chest at the thought of not seeing my family on Christmas. I was going to ask my parents to spend it in Boston, but my older brother has kids and I'm sure they'll want to see them open gifts.

Her eyes light up. "Really?"

I nod my head. "Really. Now, let's get in the shower and get all bundled up. The tree lots in Boston are even colder than the ones you're used to in New York."

She follows me as I walk to the bathroom, turning on the shower to warm it for us. "Actually, I haven't had a Christmas tree since I moved." I give her a shocked look. "What?" she shrugs. "I've been on tour for the last decade. I'm never home during the holidays. Last year, I spent the day alone in a hotel room. I think I was in Japan. I honestly can't even remember."

This fucking girl. She makes me want to give her the

whole fucking world. Starting with a proper Christmas. "Well, I guess it's fate, then," I tell her as I pull her into the shower. "Let me get you cleaned up and then we'll make some Christmas traditions of our own. Just us, and like, millions of other people once the photos get released."

I drop to my knees without a word, kissing her thighs. She giggles in response. "What are you doing?"

I look up with a mischievous grin. "Cleaning you up," I reply. She tilts her head back, resting it on the wall as I throw her leg over my shoulder and fuck her with my tongue. I've barely pulled her clit into my mouth before she goes off like a rocket, her juices coating my lips. "Holy shit, babe. That was fast," I say, licking the remnants from the inside of her thighs.

She opens her eyes, breathing still ragged. "I was so turned on from having you in my mouth."

I groan, standing up. "You can't say things like that when we have plans, Songbird. You're going to get me in trouble when there's a Christmas tree farm full of photographers waiting all alone and I've got you pinned down, coming all over me in my bed instead."

She smiles, still completely sated as I wash her hair and body before pushing her out the door to get dressed so I can clean myself without getting distracted by her tight little ass.

When we're both ready, we head out to the car, hand-in-hand. There are no cameras in the parking garage, so we don't actually have to be touching, but I don't give a fuck. I'm not letting her go anytime soon.

Two hours later, we return to my apartment with our brand-new Christmas tree in tow. It's not a real tree because when we got to the farm, Bella said she couldn't bear to cut down a tree just for it to die. So, we walked around, playing in the snow while photographers snapped photos of us. Then, we made a curbside pickup order at Target for a tree with all the decorations her little heart desired. She was all smiles on the way home, clutching her cup of hot cocoa, while we belted out Christmas songs. Well, *she* belted them out while I tried my best.

"This is the last of it," Carlo says, setting two large bags on the counter. He turns to Bella. "Your flight back to New York will be here at five this evening, so I'll leave you to it until it's time to go."

"Thank you, Carlo," she says, giving him a hug before he heads into the elevator. She turns to me, looking like a kid on, well…Christmas morning, before running over and ripping the box holding the tree wide open.

"Whoa, there," I say with a chuckle. "Let me do that. You go pick out which ornaments you want to use and I'll set the tree up. Where do you want it?" I ask. Even though it's my apartment, I want her to feel at home here. And every time I look at the tree, I want to see her as happy as she is right now.

"Hmmm," she says, tapping her plump bottom lip. "How about in that corner?" She points. "That way, we can see it when we're snuggled up on the couch."

Fuck, this feels domestic. And I don't hate it.

I get to work, setting things up as she prepares the decorations. It doesn't take long before my apartment strongly resembles Whoville. There are lights draped over everything that would stand still and there are more pink ornaments than any grown man should own, but that's what my girl wanted. And she deserves all of it.

Reaching into the bag, I grab out one last surprise. Walking over to her, I hold the mistletoe above my head as I yank her to me.

"Really, Mav? You bought a mistletoe?" She scoffs. "If you wanted to kiss me, you could've just said that."

"Okay," I shrug, throwing the bundle of holly leaves onto the couch. "I want to kiss you."

I don't give her a chance to answer before lifting her off the ground and pressing my lips to hers. She tastes like chocolate and marshmallows. And *mine*.

Although this whole day was unexpected, it couldn't have been more perfect. I'm the luckiest son of a bitch in the world, getting to make memories like these with the real Bella Simon.

ELEVEN
MAVERICK

"DOWN!" the Pittsburgh quarterback yells over his hometown crowd. "Red eighty-eight! Ready. Go!" The ball is snapped, and I shoot off the line, trying like hell to get past the blocker, but he's been getting away with holding me all day. It's the AFC championship game and we're winning. So far, it's been a hell of a lot better than last year when we fought until the last second, just to go home empty handed. The Timberwolves offensive line is in survival mode already, trying to protect their quarterback so he can make some big plays.

"Hey, Taylor," I chirp at him. "You want to grab my dick, too? Or are you all set just hanging onto my fucking jersey all day?"

He snorts a laugh. "Awww, Moran. Your little girl-friend not taking care of that tiny excuse for a penis? Sorry, I can't help you. But, hey," he gives me a cocky grin, "if you're having trouble getting her off, send her my way. I'd love to bend her over and show her what a real man's dick can do."

Red takes over my vision. Before I can stop myself, I'm

in his face, shoving him back. "Watch your fucking mouth," I seethe. Because he's a little bitch, he milks it, flopping to the ground. I see the yellow flag hit the ground out of my peripheral vision. The ref clicks the button to activate his microphone.

"Personal foul. Unnecessary roughness. Defense number ninety-nine. Fifteen-yard penalty. Automatic first down."

Fuck.

Ever since the photos of us from the Christmas tree farm last month surfaced online, all anyone can talk about is my relationship with Bella. Surprisingly, music fans and Blizzard fans alike have been pretty positive in their reactions. I'm guessing that's partly a result of us being on a winning streak since the first game she attended. I'm averaging one and a half sacks per game, which is a career high for me. But I can't take all the credit. The team has been playing their hearts out. And now that Blaze Beckham has his girl back, he's doing better than ever. When we win this one, which we will, we'll be headed to the Super Bowl. Twyla was downright giddy this morning, knowing she was one win away from the grand scheme coming to fruition. I know she hoped the Blizzard would make it to the big game, with my girl headlining the half-time show.

I line back up on the edge, coming face-to-face with Deacon Taylor. Although I have an overwhelming urge to rip him to shreds for even thinking about Bella that way, I don't want to be ejected. So, I focus on the quarterback, trying to read his body language. He starts his cadence and I see it immediately. One small diversion of his eyes toward the receiver on the opposite side of where I am lets me know exactly who his main target is.

The ball is snapped, and he rolls back. I hold off for just one second before heading toward the hole in their line that gives me a straight shot at him from behind. He never sees me coming as I wrap my arms around his torso, pulling him on top of me to avoid another penalty. I wish Bella was here to watch me, but she's stuck in New York for rehearsals. I feel like I've barely seen her this week, and when I have, it's been for planned public appearances. I haven't been inside her since last weekend and it has me wound up tight.

I miss her.

The next two downs result in no gain, giving our offense the ball back. At this point, we're just trying to keep the clock running and move enough to keep the ball in our possession. The guys are like a well-oiled machine with Tanner Lake under center. He's a mysterious fucker, but I wouldn't want anyone else leading our team. With Beckham and Davis out there with him, they're unstoppable.

The game ends with us beating Pittsburgh thirty to twenty-seven. And I'm headed to my first Super Bowl.

I can't wait to get home and celebrate with the girl who is quickly becoming the best part of my days.

BELLA

"Thanks, Carlo," I say as he opens the car door outside Maverick's building. I make my way through the revolving door, heading straight toward the elevator with my overnight bag slung over my shoulder. He just texted saying his plane just landed and he's trying to get home as fast as he can. I told him my flight from New York is running behind, but that was a lie. In fact, I made it so all my halftime show rehearsals were done early today, so I could be waiting for Mav when he arrived.

"Hey, Charlie!" I say to the elevator attendant. "How are Trish and the pups?"

"There's my favorite superstar!" he replies. "They're doing great. Max and Walter loved the homemade treats you sent. Gobbled them right up!" I've been spending a lot of time here with Maverick and have gotten to know the staff pretty well. As soon as Charlie showed me a photo of his wife holding their two French Bulldogs, I made an order for ingredients to make treats for them. Mav didn't know what to say when he found me in the kitchen with flour everywhere. But when I explained to him that I was never able to have a dog of my own because of my busy schedule, he stepped in and helped me make little Christmas packages for Charlie's fur babies. Lucky for me, the evening ended with me bent over in the shower as Maverick made sure every inch of my body was clean... and satisfied.

I step off the elevator into the dark, quiet apartment and head straight to the bedroom. I don't know how much time I have to prepare, so I shimmy out of my sweatpants and pull my shirt over my head. I reach into my bag and pull out the lingerie I picked out especially for tonight.

I step into the all-white lace bodysuit and pull the thin straps over my shoulders. The entire thing is completely sheer, my rosy nipples visible through the cups of the bodice. Ice blue garter straps hang from the bottom, where I attach my white fishnet thigh highs.

I throw my discarded clothes back into my bag and toss it into the corner of Maverick's bedroom. My nerves are on high alert as I think about him coming home to find me ready for him, wearing lingerie in his team's colors. I look at my reflection in the full-length mirror and can barely believe that I'm seeing the same girl that walked into this apartment two months ago. I was shy and inexperienced. I'll never forget the way my body shook as Maverick kissed me for the first time. While I still lack some of the confidence I long to have, he's made me feel like a sexy, powerful woman who deserves to feel good.

I trail my fingertips down my body, starting at my throat and coasting my hands lightly to my breasts. I keep my touch featherlight as I circle my nipples with the pads of my fingers and let out a harsh exhale when the tight buds begin to harden under them. I keep my left hand where it is, sliding my right one down my torso slowly, until I'm brushing over my already sensitive center. The barely-there contact has me letting out a quiet moan.

"Fuck," a deep voice whispers from behind me. I stiffen, meeting Maverick's eyes in the mirror. I didn't even hear him come in. And I have no idea how long he's been standing there.

I go to turn toward him, but I pause when he speaks again. "Keep going," he says, eyes still boring into mine through the mirror. He steps in the room, sitting down in the plush chair in the corner. He looks like a king on his throne, legs spread wide as he watches me intently. "Rub your clit, Bella."

I return my hand to my apex, using my middle finger to make soft circles over the lace. My mouth drops open as I add more pressure, pleasure building in my stomach as I do. I look back to Maverick, who is palming his cock over his dress pants as he watches me. A wave of confidence floods over me as I continue making myself feel good.

"Pull it to the side," he orders, his voice full of gravel. "Push a finger inside your cunt for me, baby." I don't hesitate as I do what he says, pulling the gusset of my body-suit to one side before sinking a finger inside my soaked pussy. I slowly pump in and out, my eyes never leaving Maverick as he unzips his pants and pulls out his beautiful cock. He spits in his hand as he strokes himself while watching me.

I turn, leaning to rest my back on the cold glass of the mirror, opening my legs more so he can see as I plunge two fingers inside my dripping heat. "Maverick, it feels so good," I moan as I throw my head back in pleasure. I continue fucking myself, my orgasm building quickly as my palm bumps against my swollen clit.

"That's it, Songbird. Finger fuck yourself for me. Come on your hand so I can lick it clean," he chokes out, stroking himself slow enough that he isn't getting what he needs. "Do a good job, baby. I'd hate to split you in two when I feed this cock into your tight pussy." I whimper at the thought of him stretching me.

Trying to prep myself for him, I add a third finger, but they don't feel like his. I can't reach the same spots he does. "Maverick, please," I beg. "I can't get there."

"You can," he replies. "And you will. I'm not fucking you until you make yourself come." I whine again, hoping he'll cave and give me what I want, but he doesn't. He just continues watching me, lazily stroking himself. His dick looks painfully hard, but he's just grazing over it with his hand.

"Come here," he says. I remove my fingers from my body and walk toward him, barely able to stay upright. He pulls his pants and boxers down his legs, kicking them to the side. "Straddle me, but don't lower down," he instructs. I obey, swinging one leg up onto the chair before settling the other one on the other side of his hips. I'm up on my knees, the head of his cock just inches from where I ache for him. "One finger. Reach around and go in from behind," he commands. I put one arm behind my back, moving my bodysuit aside and arching to get the right angle before sinking my middle finger back inside. I'm soaked, dripping into my hand as I begin pumping in and out.

Maverick uses one hand to grip my hip, holding me up while the other strokes his cock. Just as I start to get frustrated again, he pulls on himself at the perfect angle, making his tip rub against my clit. I moan at the contact, feeling my pussy tighten around my finger.

"There she is," he whispers, watching as he continues using his cock to stimulate my swollen bundle of nerves. My hips begin to rock on their own accord as I move my finger deeper, finally able to reach my g-spot. Between that and the little bit of contact Maverick is allowing me, I feel my orgasm start to pull low in my belly. My breathing becomes labored, and it isn't long before I finally feel myself heading toward the summit. I'm right there.

"Good girl, Bella. Come for me and I'll fuck you," he says. And that's all I need as I shatter above him. My hips buck and my thighs burn as I ride out my orgasm. Before I'm even fully finished, he yanks my arm away and pulls tightly on the fabric between my legs, ripping it completely at the seams before slamming into me. I see stars as he takes my hand, the one that is still coated in my cum, and sucks my fingers into his mouth.

"Oh, fuck!" I scream. I'm not sure what to focus on. The overstimulation as he fucks into me, the way he swirls his tongue around my fingers, or the sting of him stretching me. But even with all of those sensations battling each other, I continue bouncing up and down until pleasure is the only thing I feel.

"That's it," he praises. "Ride my cock. You feel so fucking good." Our heavy breaths and the sounds of our bodies crashing together fill the dark room as we fuck like wild animals. He digs both hands into my hips, lifting me up then dropping me back down, over and over.

I feel the pressure begin to build again as he uses my body for his pleasure. "Oh my God, Mav, baby—" I whine. "I think I'm going to come."

He reaches around the back of my neck, pulling me toward him and crushing our mouths together. As soon as he forces his tongue past my lips, I detonate, shaking as I have the hardest orgasm of my life. "Fuck, Bella," he growls against my lips. "You're strangling me. I can't hold it anymore." I'm barely coherent as he thrusts up one last time, pumping his hot load into me with a groan.

Neither of us move as he begins to soften inside me. As I lean forward to rest my head on his shoulder, he presses a tender kiss to my temple. I don't know how he's feeling, but none of this is fake to me anymore. If I'm honest, it never really was. From the moment I met Maverick, I knew he was different than everyone else in my life. He taught me that I deserve the things I want, and he's helped me find the confidence to take them.

I'm in love with him.

I've been struggling to push the feelings away for weeks now, but they just keep getting stronger every time I'm without him. The nights when I'm alone in bed, in my empty penthouse…those are the moments when I feel his absence. And all I want is to get back to him as fast as I can. Then, when I'm with him, I dread having to go back home. But what if it really *is* fake to him? What if he's just enjoying this thing until after Super Bowl, then he plans on moving on with his life when Twyla announces our breakup?

I can't think about any of it. I just want him to feel the things I feel. The butterflies I get in my stomach when I'm on my way to him. And the emptiness I feel when I leave. The one great thing about never having a boyfriend is that I've never had to endure a heartbreak. And I know Maverick would be worth the pain. I just hope that when I tell him he already holds my heart, he wants to keep it safe.

TWELVE
BELLA

Super Bowl Sunday

"HOW DOES IT FEEL?" Edison, my sound technician asks as he double-checks my in-ear monitor.

"It's good. Fits better than the last one," I say, shaking my head to ensure that it's a tight fit. I stand still as he wraps the small wire around the back of my head and tucks the receiver into the pocket on the back of my costume.

The second quarter just started, and the Blizzard are up by two touchdowns. I haven't been able to watch it live at all because I'm sequestered in a large room while we prepare for the halftime show. I haven't been allowed to leave since Mav dropped me off this morning when we arrived at the stadium. I'm fully dressed, equipment has been tested, and I'm about to do my vocal warmups. I'm nervous, but I don't think it has as much to do with my performance as it does with how badly I want the Blizzard to win this game.

I woke up this morning in an empty bed, the sound of

Maverick's retching coming from the bathroom. I rubbed his back as he vomited, sitting there on the floor as he explained to me that he always throws up before big games. He was a bundle of nerves all morning, only putting on a confident expression when we arrived at the stadium, walking hand-in-hand as paparazzi snapped photos and yelled questions at us.

"Bella, what songs can we expect to hear at halftime?"

"Maverick, will you be able to get through Dallas' offensive line today?"

"Are you guys in love?"

I'd love to know the answer to that last one, myself. If you're asking *me,* the answer is yes. I've known for weeks now that I'm head-over-heels for him. And I know he likes me, but he's given me no indication of how deeply his feelings run. I've been too afraid to tell him where I'm at, and way too scared to ask him about his own.

"You ready?" Sammi asks from beside me. "Have you stretched?"

I nod my head. "I've done it twice." It's a pretty action-packed performance, even more so than my normal ones, so I'm trying to stay warm for it.

"Good idea," she says. "You know, I don't think I've ever told you this, but I'm really proud of you. A couple months ago, you were passive and let everyone walk all over you. But you've changed. You've made suggestions these last few weeks during rehearsal that have made this show even better than I could've hoped. Whatever it is that's giving you this new-found confidence, keep it around. Or keep *him* around." She winks before walking toward the group of dancers on the other side of the room.

When I told Maverick about my ideas for the performance, he told me they were *badass* and encouraged me to tell Sammi we were making them happen. I went to rehearsal that day so hyped up, that her saying no was never even an option. I would've never been able to do it without him. He's made me better since I met him.

The door opens and a man with a headset pops his head in. "We're almost at the two-minute warning," he says. "We need you guys stage-ready in five minutes." He leaves as quickly as he came and I head to the corner, sitting at the piano to do my vocal warmups.

While I go through the exercises, I look up at the muted television on the wall in front of me. I've been sneaking glances since I got in here, trying to watch Maverick as he plays. The offense is on the field, but they make a stop as the clock hits the two-minute mark in the half. As the broadcast gets ready to cut to a commercial, the camera pans in on the guy I'm looking for as he puts his arms up victoriously. Fuck, he's so hot. Just seeing him and knowing he's mine, even if it's just for show, gives me the determination to hit that stage and give the performance of my life.

MAVERICK

"Let's fucking go, boys!" Dalton Davis yells as we head to the locker room. I look around nervously, trying to figure out how I can sneak away to watch Bella sing. It's frowned upon by the league for any of us to be on the field during halftime, but I'm desperate to see her, even if it's from afar.

The team shuffles into the room and guys take their places on the benches in front of their lockers while Coach Mills starts his speech. Since we're winning, it's mostly just praising us for our hard work and going over some of the things we need to watch out for in the second half. But

I'm not fucking listening. I'm just waiting for him to turn his back so I can slip out the door.

The length of halftime for the Super Bowl is thirty minutes, as opposed to the thirteen minutes we are used to, so I'm hoping we'll be done here soon.

"Okay," Coach says, clapping his hands. "Take some time to relax and recover. Anyone caught out of this room will be dealing with me after the game, win or lose." He turns, walking into the office with the other coaches to go over their plan for the second half.

Fuck.

I'm a ball of nerves, bouncing my knees, hating the fact that Bella is about to walk on stage and I'm not there. I just need to see her.

"Hey, Moran," our quarterback, Tanner Lake, says. I look up at him, hoping he doesn't see the anxiety written all over my face. The last thing I need is for my captain to think my head isn't in the game. "Can I see you in the hall for a second?"

I look at him, confused. "But Coach said—"

He waves me off. "It's okay. I just want to talk to you privately for a couple minutes. If he says anything, I'll tell him I said it was alright."

"Yeah," I say, forcing out an exhale as I stand and follow him out the door. I shut it behind me, expecting him to turn around, but he just heads back toward the tunnel. "Ummm," I say. "Where are we going?" He says nothing as he leads me to the edge of the field, where the entire stage is visible. We stand there and watch together as the lights dim and Bella steps out.

As soon as I see her, I stop breathing. She is perfection in her sequined blue costume, fringes barely hitting her upper thighs. Thighs that I've rested my head on as she played with my hair while we watched a movie. Her hands grip her bedazzled microphone as she takes in the crowd. Hands that I've held as we slept, unable to fully relax without touching her somehow. She smiles and the crowd goes wild. For her.

For *my girl.*

Fuck. I love her.

I love her so much it hurts. This whole thing was supposed to be fake, but I think it started blooming into something real the first night she stayed at my house. When she had that nightmare, I was overcome with fear thinking she was hurt. I should've known she was already finding a place in my heart. It was the last thing I expected when Twyla told me about her plan, but here I am, watching my Songbird captivate the entire country with her voice.

I look over at Tanner, eyes wide with realization. "I love her," I say, tasting the words as they move across my tongue. "I fucking *love* Bella Simon."

His expression softens. "Congrats, man. Take good care of her."

"Thank you, Lake," I reply. For helping me get out here. For knowing how much it meant to me. For leading the Blizzard, on and off the field.

I look back to the stage. The first song is over, and the dancers are hitting every move in sync as the band plays, but Bella is nowhere to be seen. I watch as the stage goes black before a spotlight illuminates a small area. Just then, the floor opens, and she slowly rises up from underneath. The music is loud, and the fans are screaming, but I can't hear any of it. My heart whooshes loudly in my ears as I see that she's changed her costume. Now, she's wearing only a Blizzard jersey. *My* jersey. My last name and number ninety-nine stretches across her back as she turns, pausing dramatically as she allows the crowd to take it in.

She's claiming me. In my stadium. On my field.

This has to be real.

I stand in awe as she commands the stage, never missing a beat as fireworks go off all around her. There are eighty-thousand people in this room, but the only one I see is her. She's so beautiful and talented. There's no way this thing ends in any other way than her being mine for the rest of our lives.

Now I just need to win this game so I can tell her.

THIRTEEN
MAVERICK

CONFETTI RAINS down over us as the clock hits double zeros. The Boston Blizzard won the Super Bowl. And all I can think about is getting Bella into my arms.

I search around the field frantically as friends and family members of my teammates rush to congratulate them. Blaze Beckham's girlfriend Mads blows past me, jumping into his arms while a dark-haired woman trails her, giving Dalton Davis a quick hug before backing away, her cheeks reddening. I continue searching the crowd for Bella and stop in my tracks as Carlo's salt and pepper hair catches my eye. Just then, a blonde blur comes into view, whipping past her bodyguard, running straight at me. She jumps up and I catch her, lifting her in the air as she laughs.

"You won!" she screams. "I'm so proud of you! You were amaz—" I cut her off by crashing my lips to hers. She wraps her legs around my waist, opening her mouth as we shamelessly make out while cameras flash all around us.

I reluctantly pull back, one hand under her ass as the other cups her cheek. "Baby, your performance...it was fucking perfection. And you in my jersey? I've never seen anything sexier." I smile.

Her brows raise in surprise. "You saw it? But how?"

I look over at Tanner, who stands alone as he watches us. "I had a little help sneaking out," I say with a wink in his direction. He gives me a quick nod and turns away as I bring my focus back to my girl. "Bella, I have to tell you something. I lov—"

"Here she comes!" Dalton yells, smacking me on the shoulder. I look to where he's pointing as the NFL commissioner makes his way through the crowd with the Lombardi trophy. Players wait their turn to kiss it as it passes by. Unsanitary? Probably. But it's tradition and we're all too hyped up to care.

Bella drops her legs and slides down my body before giving me one quick peck on the lips. "Go. We'll talk later."

I nod my head because this definitely isn't the time to confess my feelings. I'll get her alone and tell her that I'm a man obsessed before making love to her for the first time as my real girlfriend. Am I cocky? No. I just know we're inevitable. I can feel it in my soul.

"Where's Carlo?" I ask, lifting my head to look for him. As if he heard me, his head pops up from the crowd. I lead Bella by the hand over to him, only turning toward my team when his arm goes protectively around her shoulders as he leads her to safety.

I make my way to the trophy, touching it with my hand as it passes by. I want Bella's lips to be the last thing on mine, not some piece of metal. She's the real prize. This whole season, all I cared about was winning this game. I never expected the win to come in second place to the feeling of falling in love with Bella Simon. She's my whole world. All the other stuff is just the cherry on top of an amazing year.

I watch proudly as my teammates take the stage, making speeches to thank their families, friends, and the fans. Tanner accepts his Most Valuable Player award, which he rightfully earned today. After the trophies are given and we've all done our on-field interviews, I head toward the locker room and jump in the shower. The excitement is still thick in the air as I wrap a towel around my waist, hurrying to my locker. I just want to get dressed and get back to Bella so we can congratulate each other properly.

"Hey, Mr. Defensive Player of the Year," Dalton says, causing me to whip around with my brows furrowed in confusion. "Get your girl. We're going to Vegas!"

"I'm going to need you to repeat that," I say.

He winks. "Plane's all ready for us at the airport. Let's get fucked up!" he yells, earning a collective cheer from around the room.

"Repeat the first part, dickhead," I say. "It sounded like you called me DPOY."

"Yep," he says. "Maybe if you hadn't rushed off to the showers, you'd have heard the announcement. Congrats, bro." He slaps me on the shoulder.

Holy shit.

I got the ring, the highest honor for a defensive player, and I'm about to get the girl. It's good to be Maverick Moran.

"So," he says. "Put your dick away, grab Bella, and let's jet, baby. The night is young!"

I get dressed and text her.

MAVERICK: Hey baby, let's go to Vegas.

BELLA: And kiss the single life good-bye? LOL

MAVERICK: Actually...

BELLA: Mav, don't tease me.

MAVERICK: *wink emoji* Some of the guys are taking a private plane to Vegas. Wanna go?

BELLA: I mean, technically I'm a free woman. I can do whatever I want.

BELLA: Let's do it!

MAVERICK: That's my girl! Meet me by the car in fifteen. Tell Carlo to put the divider up and crank the tunes so I can eat you out on the way to the airport.

BELLA: *melting emoji*

BELLA

We board the plane and Maverick pulls me into his lap on the plush leather seat before burying his face in my neck. I giggle at the contact, but a small moan leaves my lips as his tongue traces my throat. He looks up before kissing me deeply. I should care, considering there are about ten other people on the plane with us, but I just can't get enough of him.

"You taste like me," I whisper, memories of how

quickly he made me come on his tongue in the car resurfacing, making my clit throb with need.

"You like how your cunt tastes, baby?" he asks quietly.

I exhale a shaky breath as I nod my head.

"Fuck, Bella," he groans. "Keep that shit up and you'll be a member of the Mile High Club."

I giggle, looking up to see Blaze Beckham pulling his girlfriend into the bathroom, the door slamming shut behind them. "Well, that idea's out. Looks like Blaze has the same idea for Mads." Just then, we hear a loud crack followed by a feminine moan coming from that direction.

My eyes widen and Maverick laughs. "Let them have their fun. They've been through a lot."

"Get it, girl!" her best friend Dia yells as she plops down in the seat next to Dalton Davis. She looks at me and smiles.

I look around to see his teammates and friends having the time of their lives and my heart squeezes. These are the types of friends I want in my life. People who are just there for each other. No pretenses, no expectations from one another. The season is officially over and they're still choosing to spend time with each other.

An hour later, we step off the plane into the cars that await to bring us to our hotel. Carlo has been amazing, stepping back and letting Maverick take care of me. He's made sure all my destinations are secure and he's agreed to watch me from afar while I enjoy my first night of real freedom. I think he knows I'm safe with Mav, too.

We pull into the private parking garage of our hotel and walk inside as a group. Everyone has been indulging in champagne and shots, some more than others, and we're loud as hell on our way to the bar.

The hostess greets us as we enter, opening a velvet rope for us to pass through. "Congratulations on your win!" she says to the guys before turning to me. "And your performance was the best I've ever seen."

"Thank you," I say as Maverick grabs my hand and leads me to the VIP section that has been cleared out for us.

Mads and Dia run up to us, taking my hands and pulling me along with them. "Sorry, Mav," Mads says. "We're stealing your girl." He reaches for me, but they're quick as they wrench my arms away and we take off to order drinks.

"Okay, don't take this the wrong way," Dia says. "But Maverick is so fucking hot. His quads are bigger than my head. Have you ever just…licked them?"

I throw my head back in a laugh. "I don't blame you for thinking that. And, yes, I've pretty much licked him everywhere." My face heats with embarrassment, but I'm quickly validated when Mads puts her hand up for a high-five, which I immediately indulge. The fact that I can just be myself around them isn't something I've gotten to experience much. I always have to be careful what I say because I've been taught that nobody can be trusted. But I know it's different with Maverick's friends. They're kind and genuine.

The bartender hands us our shots and we hold them up. "To getting in trouble," Mads says.

Dia groans. "For the love of God, Madison. Do *not* get that man worked up. I'm supposed to room with you guys tonight."

"What's done is done," Mads says with a wink before downing her tequila and slamming the glass on the bar. "See ya." She waves at us before turning and walking to the dance floor as we throw back our shots.

"Ugh," Dia whines, setting her glass down. "Looks like I'm sleeping in the hallway tonight."

Confusion takes over my face. "Why?"

Before she can answer me, a strong set of arms wraps around my waist. I take in the scent of Mav's cologne before glancing over my shoulder at him. "Sorry, Dia. I need my girl back," he says, kissing my cheek.

"Yeah, yeah," she replies, rolling her eyes. "You're all fucking gorgeous, and everyone is getting laid but me. Fuck you guys," she mumbles sarcastically before walking back toward our section where Dalton and Tanner sit, watching over the crowd.

I turn toward him, wrapping my arms around his neck. "I think I love your friends."

He cups my cheek with his hand, leaning his mouth to my ear. "I think I love *you*."

I still in his arms, pulling back to look into his eyes. I need to know if he's serious. I expect to see a teasing expression on his face, but all I see is a hopeful smile. "Can we go somewhere quiet?" he asks.

I nod my head because suddenly, I can't think of anything else I'd rather do than hear him repeat himself where I can soak in every last word. He takes me by the hand, interlocking our fingers as he leads me to the private elevators that take us to the floor of executive suites Tanner booked for our group. I follow him wordlessly as we reach our room, and he uses the key card to unlock our door. As soon as we're inside, he turns, lifting me off my feet and pressing me against the door. I wrap my legs around him, feeling his erection press against my clit as he grinds into me.

"Baby," he groans, trailing his lips down my neck, sucking on the sensitive skin under my ear. "I need to be inside you right now."

"Maverick. P-please," I beg. I've never needed him so bad. My whole body prickles with anticipation as he carries me to the bed, gently laying me down before lowering himself onto me. I open my legs, the fabric of the long jersey I just couldn't take off after my performance bunching above my hips. He grinds into me, the pressure from his cock making a direct hit to my sensitive clit as I feel my body begin to tighten with my building orgasm.

"These fucking shorts," he growls, pulling my shorts and panties down in one go and throwing them across the room. He frantically brings his hands to the button of his dress pants, pulling them down with his boxer briefs, making his impressive dick spring free. My mouth waters at the sight of it.

I move to sit up so I can take him into my mouth, but he pushes me back. "Bella, I'm hanging by a fucking thread right now. If you even breathe on my cock, I swear I'll blow all over your pretty face. And I *need* to be inside you."

I gasp as he lowers his hand, spearing two fingers inside me. "Fuck, baby. You're dripping," he says, pumping them in and out slowly.

"Maverick," I whimper. "Please fuck me."

In an instant, he replaces his fingers with his dick, filling me and stretching me to my absolute limit. He stills, waiting for my inner walls to relax before he begins slowly thrusting in and out. I feel him *everywhere*. Inside my body, heart, and soul. It's almost overwhelming as he continues fucking into me.

He kisses me softly before pressing his forehead to mine. "Tell me it's real, baby. Tell me you feel it, too," he begs. *"Please."*

My heart cracks at the desperation in his voice. My whole body is shivering with adrenaline as I nod my head, tears filling my eyes. "I feel it," I whisper.

"Fuck," he lets out a breath of relief. "I love you."

"I love you so much, Maverick," I reply as he picks up his pace, my orgasm barreling toward me.

"I'm so close," he pants. "I need to feel you come on my cock, Bella." A few more hard punches of his hips and I'm coming apart under him, my legs shaking as black takes over my vision. I'm barely coming down as I hear his loud grunt as he releases into me with jerky movements.

He slows, passionately kissing me for what seems like hours as he softens inside me. "That was incredible," he whispers before carefully pulling out, watching as a mixture of our cum leaks onto the bed. Just like he always does, he uses his finger to push it back in, unable to let a single drop go to waste.

"One day, I'm going to put a baby in you," he says, like it's the most natural thing in the world. I gasp at his words, but he just winks before dropping another quick kiss to my lips.

Reluctantly, he gets up, walking to the bathroom and returning to the bed with a warm cloth. I let him clean me before pulling him back up next to my sated body on the bed. He hums contentedly as he cuddles behind me, pulling me into his chest.

"Fuuuuuckkkk," he groans, running a hand down his face.

"What?" I ask, concerned.

"Which one of us is telling Twyla to cancel the breakup announcement?"

FOURTEEN
MAVERICK

I WAKE up to a loud screeching sound filling the room. "What the fuck is that?" I grumble, pulling Bella's warm body into mine.

She giggles, trying to pull away, but lucky for me, I'm a lot stronger than she is. "It's your phone."

"Mmmm," I say into her hair. "Whoever it is can fuck right off. It's the offseason." The ringing stops but starts back up immediately. I throw a little tantrum, complete with a couple playful kicks to the mattress before reaching over Bella's body and face-planting into her tits. "Can you grab that for me, baby?" I mumble, barely audibly, into her soft skin, earning a breathy laugh as I feel her reach over to the nightstand.

"It's Twyla," she says, panicked. I have no idea why she's worried. Bella and I have been spending nights together for the past couple months and nobody has said a word. Even if Twyla still assumes it's fake between us, we're only doing what she asked us to do. We're looking like a believable couple.

I look up at Bella to find that her eyes are as wide as

saucers and her face is pale. "Should we tell her now that we're really together? Do you think she already *knows?* Oh my God, she's going to hate us for going rogue!"

I chuckle at her rambling. "Babe, how would she know? Plus, who cares if she does? What's she going to do? Ground us?" I say as I press the button to answer the call, putting it on speakerphone. "Hello?"

"How's my Defensive Player of the Year?" she sings. Fuck. I almost forgot about that. I was too excited about things becoming real between Bella and me.

"I'm pretty damn good," I reply proudly.

"Well," she begins, and I already know I'm not going to like this conversation. She's definitely going to make me get out of bed. "Don't be mad," Yep. I knew it. "I scheduled you an interview with Tailgate Media for this evening during their five o' clock live show."

I wince. "Please tell me I can do it remotely from this hotel room without having to put on pants."

"Sorry," she says. "They want you live in the studio. The good news is that the interview is with Madison Rodgers, so Blaze will be there. And Tanner will be going as well since he won the Super Bowl MVP award. I arranged for a private plane to take you all back to Boston in two hours."

Fuck.

"Okay," I relent. As much as I would like to stay in this bed, wrapped up in Bella for the rest of the day, I have to remember how hard I worked to get this honor. I knew there would be lots of attention and interviews, and I need to embrace them.

She continues. "Have you seen Bella? I know she was in Vegas with you guys, but I texted her a bunch of times and she hasn't replied."

Bella shakes her head frantically beside me, mouthing *no* over and over. But what's the point in lying? "She's right here. Do you want to talk to her?" I ask.

There's a pause. "You guys know you don't have to keep making people think you're a couple, right? If you want the breakup to be believable, you can start going places without the other. Then we can just say you grew apart."

Abso-fucking-lutely not. I just got her. There's no way I'm letting the world think we aren't together.

"Actually," I say, ready to lay it all out for her. "Bella and I—"

The phone is yanked from my hand before I can finish my sentence. "Hey, Twyla!" Bella says, fake excitement lacing her tone. "What's up?"

"Oh, hi," she replies. "I was going to tell you that I arranged for a separate plane to take you back to New York this afternoon. I figured you'd want to go home. You know, since you're free to do whatever your little heart desires now." Bella looks at me and I take her hand, giving her a soft smile in silent support. "Just go to the airport with Maverick, then you can go your separate ways."

"Umm, okay," Bella says before they finish the call. She sets the phone down, turning to me. "I don't want to go back to New York," she whines, her pouty bottom lip trembling.

I pull her into a hug. "Then don't. Come stay with me in Boston until you decide how you want to spend your break. I have nothing but time for the next couple of months, so I'll follow you like a little puppy, or I'll wait at home for you to come back from your adventures. Whatever you want, I'll give it to you. For now, I'll go home to Boston and get this interview done. You go to New York, pack up what you need, and meet me at home later tonight." *Home.* I love the sound of that.

She melts into my embrace. "I don't know why I didn't just let you tell her," she sighs. "I'm not used to breaking the rules. I always do what I'm told. It's my beige flag," she says, scrunching her nose.

I laugh, "It's fine, baby. We'll tell her together. Anyway, this is *her* fault. She came up with this plan. She should've known you'd fall for my good looks and charm." I wink. "And my huge dick."

"Oh my God, Mav," she gasps as she playfully slaps my chest. I can't help myself, so I pin her down to the bed, tickling her until she can barely breathe before kissing her passionately.

"I love you, Songbird."

"I love you, too." She gets off the bed, attempting to pull me behind her, but I outweigh her by over a hundred pounds, so I pull her back on top of me for another kiss before I stand us both up.

"I guess we'd better hurry. We've got some planes to catch."

FIFTEEN
BELLA

"HAS anyone heard from Dalton or Dia?" Tanner asks as we make our way through the airport's private entrance.

"I texted with Dia earlier," Mads replies as Blaze unabashedly kisses her neck like we aren't here. Those two are sickeningly sweet. "She said she was tired and that she was going to catch a later flight. Dalton didn't want her to have to fly alone, so he's waiting with her."

Blaze looks up. "I can't believe she's letting him anywhere near her. And she was almost being nice to him last night. It was weird."

Maybe she didn't sleep alone in the hallway, after all.

"Come here, Songbird," Maverick says as he pulls me in for a hug. Sadness grips at my heart like a vice. I know we'll only be apart until tonight, but now that we've told each other how we feel, even a day feels like an eternity. My plan is simple. Go back to my place, pack as much of my stuff as I can, and head straight to Boston. Mav will be done with his interview by the time I get there, and we can do whatever we want for the next couple of months. He drops his lips to mine, and I savor the way he tastes.

"I am painfully single right now," Tanner mumbles from between the four of us. I actually find it hard to believe because he seems like such a great guy. And he's hot as sin, too. It's only a matter of time before he's off the market, I'm sure.

We say our final goodbyes and Maverick leads me to the door where my plane awaits, kissing me one last time. "Fly safe, baby. I love you."

"I love you, too," I reply, still getting butterflies at the thought of finally saying it out loud. "I'll see you tonight."

I board the plane, emptiness hollowing my chest at the lack of proximity between us. All I can focus on is getting everything done as fast as I can and getting back to him. As I settle in my seat, the pilot approaches me. "Good morning, Miss Simon. My name is Annette and I'll be your pilot today."

"Nice to meet you, Annette," I say. She's an older woman, maybe in her late fifties with grey sprinkled in her dark brown hair. Our regular pilot, Richard, is taking some time off to enjoy his new granddaughter, so I thought it would be a good time to add a female pilot to our team. Thankfully, we found one with Air Force flight experience. I know I'm safe in her capable hands.

She briefs me on the flight, explaining that there is a possible ice storm passing through New York this afternoon, but she's hoping to miss it. If we do, the flight will be about four and a half hours, which gives me plenty of time to get everything done and be on my way to Boston this evening.

I buckle up and prepare for takeoff, putting my phone in airplane mode, making sure I'm connected to the WiFi. I notice my battery is only about three-quarters of the way full. In my hurry to pack this morning, I accidentally left my charger in the hotel room. We won't be in the air that long. It should be fine.

I pull my bag up onto the mahogany table in front of me and dig through for my AirPods, finding them buried under the mess that I never have time to clean. Putting them into my ears, I pull up the audiobook I've been listening to. It's a rom com about a hockey player who accidentally gets his goalie's younger sister pregnant. She just threw up in his shoe and I'm doing my best not to cackle out loud.

A little over four hours later, the flight attendant approaches me. The turbulence has been getting worse in the last thirty minutes and I've been doing my best to focus on my book instead of my possible impending doom. I wouldn't say I'm a nervous flyer, but I still get anxious with the way these smaller planes can get jarred around in the air. Plus, I hate thunderstorms.

I pull out my AirPods so she knows she has my attention. "I'm sorry, Miss Simon," she says. "New York City has grounded all flights due to inclement weather, so we are going to make an emergency landing in Scranton, Pennsylvania to wait out the storm. The wind and rain are getting too bad to safely continue."

I nod my head, but I'm internally panicking. What if we crash? What if the runway is slippery? *Oh my God, what if Maverick's plane hits the bad weather?* All these questions play over and over in my mind as I pick up my phone with shaking hands and pull up our text thread.

> BELLA: We have to make an emergency landing in Scranton. I'll call you as soon as I can.

Just as I hit send, my phone dies. *Fuck*. I'll just buy a portable charger when we get to the airport.

Gripping tightly to the armrests, I prepare to land in the wind and rain.

MAVERICK

"Please," I beg the pilot. "My girlfriend is in trouble, and I need to get to Scranton. I know you can re-route us."

He gives me a sympathetic look. "Mr. Moran, I understand your concern, but it's not on our flight route and it wouldn't be smart to fly into rainy weather unnecessarily. I'm sorry."

"Thanks," I grumble, as he turns back toward the cockpit.

I'm terrified for Bella's safety after receiving her text. I've replied about a hundred times, trying to figure out what's going on, but she hasn't said a word. Even my calls are going to her voicemail. They could just be landing because they can't get into New York. Or there could be an actual emergency. It doesn't make sense that I can't get ahold of her. If it were just a routine landing to wait out the weather in New York, she'd be answering me. Updating me. Every bad scenario runs through my head as I fist my hands into my hair and tug. I just need to know she's okay.

As I begin to spiral, my phone rings. I grab it off the table quickly, hoping to see Bella's name, but it's Twyla. "Tell me she's safe," I bark into the receiver.

"What? Who?" she replies, confused.

"Bella!" I yell. "She texted saying they were making an emergency landing and now she isn't answering my calls and texts. I need to know she's ok." My hands are shaking as I stand and start pacing the aisle. Out of the corner of my eye, I see Tanner getting up from his seat and heading toward the front of the plane, but I'm too busy freaking the fuck out to see where he's going.

"Maverick, relax. I'm sure she's fine," she says, her nonchalance pissing me the fuck off.

I seethe. "Twyla, I fucking *love her*. For real. This isn't fucking fake anymore. I need to know she's safe! *Now!*" I don't normally raise my voice to her, but her dismissal is making me fume. I feel like a wild animal, and nobody is listening to me.

"Okay," she says, her voice softening. "I'll find her for you. It's going to be alright. Let me make some calls."

"Thank you," I say, nerves making my voice break as I end the call and wait for someone to tell me that Bella is safe.

SIXTEEN
BELLA

"WHAT DO YOU MEAN, I can't get off the plane?" I ask the flight attendant as we sit, unmoving, on the runway. We've been sitting here almost an hour and I just want to get off.

She gives me a sympathetic look. "Because of all the grounded flights in New York, there's more traffic here than normal. Security is concerned about the risks associated with you going into the airport. They weren't prepared for you." I curse myself for telling Carlo to take an earlier flight so I could have him ready to get me home when I got to JFK. Now I'm stuck on this plane while we wait for the green light to take off again.

"Are there any extra iPhone chargers on the plane?" I ask. "I'm sure my boyfriend is worried, and I want to let him know I'm on the ground and safe."

She scrunches her nose. "I don't think so, but let me ask."

"Thank you," I say as she turns and walks toward the front of the plane. I think for a split second that I could just ask one of the staff to use their phones, but thanks to the digital age, I don't know any phone numbers off the top of my head. So, I sit back in my seat and close my eyes. I take a few calming breaths, but I can't stop the worry that washes over me when I remember that Maverick could've been flying into bad weather, too.

I'm startled when the flight attendant returns. "Unfortunately, I couldn't find an iPhone charger, but the co-pilot has to go inside because the rain is messing with the radio connection, so he's going to see if he can get you one in there."

I let out a sigh of relief. "Thank you so much," I say as the co-pilot opens the passenger exit and waits for the airstairs to lower. He nods his head once before leaving the plane. My knee bounces as I'm left alone to worry about Maverick and how I'll get home to him. I miss him so much already. My stomach twists as I think about it, and I can't help the moisture that fills my eyes.

I try to collect myself, blinking rapidly with my head tilted up to combat the tears that are threatening to run down my cheeks.

"Sir, I can't let you on the plane," says a male voice from outside.

"Fuck you! I need to see my girlfriend!"

I jump from my seat, running to the door to see Maverick shoving past the co-pilot and taking the stairs two at a time. I'm stunned silent, unable to move as I try to figure out if what I'm seeing is real. He walks through the door, and I look up at him, blinking but still not able to form words. He closes the space between us in two large steps and grabs ahold of my face before crashing his mouth to mine. When his tongue pushes forcefully against my lips, I open for him, letting him take what he needs. His hands slide down my body, gripping my waist tightly as he ends the kiss, but leaves his lips hovering over mine.

"You're—you're here," I stammer, breathlessly. "How are you here?"

"You scared the shit out of me, baby," he says against my mouth. "I was worried sick when I couldn't get ahold of you."

I give him an apologetic look. "My phone died. I left my charger in Vegas. I'm so sorry."

He kisses my forehead, letting his lips linger before pulling away to look at me. "I don't care. I'm just glad you're safe." His arms tighten around me and that's exactly how I feel. *Safe.*

Our bubble is popped as voices fill the cabin. I look over to see Blaze, Mads, and Tanner. "Oh my God," I laugh. "You're all here!" I wiggle out of Mav's tight embrace, running over and giving them each a hug. I turn back to Maverick. "You didn't answer my question. How are you here?"

He nods at Tanner. "Ask him."

I look back over. Tanner smiles coyly as he shrugs his shoulders. "I convinced the pilot to re-route our plane. It's not a big deal."

"He bribed him with season tickets," Blaze quips, making me laugh. A feeling of warmth washes over me as I realize that they put themselves in potential danger to get to me. For the last ten years, I've wondered if the people around me were there for the right reasons. It was always a lingering thought that they were only spending time with me because I had something they could benefit from. I went through life never truly having friends that I could trust. But, with Maverick's friends, I have that. I don't have to wonder what their intentions are. They like me for me.

Mav grabs my hand and yanks me into his lap as he sits down. I giggle when he buries his face into my neck, inhaling my scent before sucking at my skin gently. I can't help but turn and kiss his plump lips again, feeling so happy to be in his arms.

"Sorry, folks," Annette says from the front of the plane. "Looks like we'll be stuck here tonight. You may want to make arrangements for lodging. The airport has a car waiting to take you wherever you need to go. We should have the go-ahead to head back to New York by morning."

"Boston," I say to her. "I'd like to go straight to Boston with my friends." I turn to see a soft expression on Mads' face from where she's cuddled into Blaze.

"Okay, then," she replies before heading back into the cockpit while I gather my things and stuff them into my bag.

"Sorry, guys," I say to them. "I know you had plans for the evening. And now you're stuck in the middle of Pennsylvania because of me."

Mads scoffs. "First of all, I love *The Office*. This place was on my bucket list. Secondly, think of it as our first real adventure as friends," she winks. I give her a genuine smile before we all make our way down the steps and into the waiting car.

MAVERICK

I use the key to open the motel door, praying it isn't a complete dump. With all the grounded flights re-routed here, it wasn't easy to find a room at all. Let alone three of them. Thankfully, this place had the accommodations for our whole group and is close to the airport, so we can get back as soon as the rain lets up.

I flip the light switch and I'm shocked as shit with the room. It certainly isn't a penthouse suite at the Bellagio, but it's clean, modern, and smells good. It'll do for a night of sleep with Bella.

Not sure how much sleeping we'll be doing, but whatever.

Ever since I found her safe and sound on that plane, my emotions have been all over the place. I'm relieved that she's not hurt or dead, but my blood is still boiling with the thought that something could've happened to her, and I wasn't there to protect her. One thing I know for certain is that I won't be letting her leave my side for a long, long time. I can't lose her. I wouldn't fucking survive it.

"Come here, baby," I say, beckoning her over with a crook of my finger. She drops her bag on the floor where she stands and saunters my way. I don't miss the extra swing in her hips as she moves. *Fuck, I can't wait to be inside her.*

As soon as she's within reach, I yank the hem of her shirt until our bodies are pressed together. Tilting her chin up with my fingers, I forcefully take her mouth with mine. She gasps and I take the opportunity to plunge my tongue inside, licking at her everywhere. I bring my hand behind her head, gripping her hair so she can't move while I continue kissing the breath from her body. She winces in pain, but the moan that follows tells me she doesn't want me to stop. Now that I have her here, I feel frenzied and wild as I grind against her toned body. I want her to feel me everywhere.

I let go of her hair so I can slide my hands around her, gripping her ass tightly, spreading her cheeks under her leggings. When I slip a finger between them, enough to put pressure on her puckered bud, she moans again.

"Do you trust me?" I ask her.

She's panting, barely able to catch her breath. "You know I do."

I pause for a moment, wanting to make sure she doesn't change her mind. But when she pulls off her leggings and thong, throws them aside, and gets on the bed on her hands and knees, that's all the green light I need.

"Fuuuuuuck, baby," I breathe. "Such a good girl, giving your holes to me." I fist my hard cock over my sweats and walk to my bag, grabbing the small bottle of lube I keep in there for those cold, lonely nights on the road. Setting it aside, I crawl up behind her on the bed and drop my mouth to her pussy. "You taste so good, Bella," I tell her as I run my tongue between her swollen lips. She tastes like heaven and sin all at once and I can't get enough of it. Of *her*.

As I push my tongue all the way into her, my nose nudges against her back hole and her pussy clenches around me. "Do you like that, baby?" I ask. "You like when I put pressure on this tight little asshole of yours?" I use my hands to spread her cheeks so I can get in closer, running my tongue from her clit to her ass, taking my time to lick and flick at it.

"Yes," she whispers. "I want more."

I'm practically shaking with anticipation and anxiety as I grab the bottle of lube from beside her and cover my fingers in it. I carefully spread it over her puckered bud, massaging the skin around it as I prepare her. "Bella, tell me to stop if it's too much. I don't want to hurt you, okay?"

"You won't," she says, pressing her face into the mattress. "But I promise I'll tell you if I need you to stop."

When I slowly sink my finger into her, her muscles tighten, trying to push me out. "Baby, I need you to relax for me." I bring my free hand up to gently rub her lower back, and I feel the tension melt from her body. I take the opportunity to push my finger in further, this time with less resistance once I breach the tight ring of muscle. "Good girl, baby. Look at you, taking my finger. It's so hot." I begin thrusting in and out and she continues slowly relaxing and opening up for me. By the time I push in a second finger, she's moaning and gripping the sheets beside her.

I lean back down, sucking her clit into my mouth while I fuck her. Her legs begin to shake, and I know she's close. I feel like I could come in my pants without even touching my dick, just from the sounds she's making.

"Mav," she whines. "I want you to—" she stops.

"What do you want, baby? Just say it and I'll give it to you."

She takes a deep breath and I slow my fingers as I wait for her response.

"I want you to fuck my ass."

Oh, fuck.

I exhale a shaky breath. "Bella, we can't. I'm too big. I've never been able to do that before. I *will* hurt you." As much as I want to say yes, I can't do it. I'll never forgive myself if I cause her pain.

She turns her head, looking at me. "Can we try? I want one of your firsts. You have so many of mine. *Please*?" She's right. She's given me so much these past couple of months. And now she's trusting me with this.

I think it over before answering her. "Okay, we'll try.

But you need to tell me if it hurts, baby. Please, promise me."

She lays her head back down on the bed. "I promise."

I remove my sweats and boxers before grabbing the lube and squeezing a very generous amount into my hand, working it all over my erection. I'm so fucking hard; I don't even think this will work. I take more lube and return two fingers to her before pressing them in until she's loose and slippery for me. My instinct is to slam in and fuck her until I come, but I know I have to be careful with her. Lining my dick up to her back hole, I slowly start to push my hips forward. Immediately, she tightens, but I keep putting pressure on her until she swallows the head of my cock. It's so tight, I can barely breathe.

"Fuck, baby. You're so tight. I'm going to pass the fuck out," I say with a strangled breath. "Are you alright?"

She nods her head into the mattress. "Go in further," she grits out.

She grips the sheet until her knuckles are white as I try to push in more, but she's too tight. "Bella, I need you to bear down for me, okay? I've got you," I reassure her. "Let me in." She follows my instruction and I'm able to go in a few more inches. Even though I'm barely halfway, it feels so fucking good. I decide this is as far as I'm going before I pull back and thrust forward just as deep.

I literally might pass out.

I slowly fuck her, trying not to blow my load before she comes. Reaching around, I rub tight circles on her clit while I continue moving inside her. "I love you so much, baby. You're taking me so well," I praise. "I'm so proud of you."

"Mav," she chokes out. "I think I'm going to—" Before she can even finish her sentence, she detonates, her muscles strangling me almost to the point of pain as she does.

"That's it, Bella. Fucking come for me," I say as I pick up speed, working her through her orgasm. She collapses forward and I continue rutting into her like a man possessed as I feel fire starting in my core and spreading throughout my limbs. Just as I'm about to come, I pull out, stroking myself onto her lower back until I have nothing left to give. I look down at her shaking body, covered in my seed and I can't help but feel an air of possessiveness pass through me. I run my hand through the warm liquid, smearing it into her skin. Marking her as mine.

I fall onto the bed, careful not to jar her as I roll her to her side and pull her back tightly to my front. I kiss her head and tell her how incredible she is until we've both caught our breath. I know she's going to be sore, so I head to the bathroom and start the hot shower before returning to the bed and carrying her back in there. I try my best to support her tired body as I gently wash her.

When she's able to stand on her own, she looks up at me. "Thank you,"

I chuckle. "Are you thanking me for fucking your ass?"

"Yeah, I guess I am," she says with a giggle. "Thank you for being someone I can trust. I never have to worry about you hurting me because I know you won't." She leans into me, wrapping her arms tightly around my waist, and my entire world shifts.

She's it for me.

What was supposed to be fake, never really was. Bella Simon had my heart from the moment I met her. I thought my priorities were straight. All I wanted was to be the best football player the Boston Blizzard had ever seen. I spent my life training and working hard to achieve that goal. I wanted the trophy and the ring. *That* was my end game. Until her.

Now, I just want to spend the rest of my life showing her how special she is. How she deserves to be loved. It might've started as a stunt, but it ended up being the realest thing I've ever done.

SEVENTEEN
BELLA

MAVERICK TAKES my hand as we head past the reception desk toward Twyla's office. I can hear her yelling before we even make it to the room.

Mav was right. She is kind of scary.

We wait in the doorway, only stepping in when she quietly points to the chairs on the opposite side of her desk. Maverick pulls out my chair before sitting down as we wait uncomfortably while she lays into whatever poor soul is on the other end of the call.

"No, you listen to me, *Sharon*," she spits. "The deal is off until you people get your shit together. Don't be surprised when your company goes under after I tell everyone how out of control you are,"

My eyes widen as I look over at Maverick, finding the same expression on his face. *Big yikes.*

She continues. "Yeah, well, I hope you sleep well at night knowing that your clients could end up losing their homes so you can make an extra buck." She hangs up, tossing the phone onto her desk. "Asswads," she mumbles before remembering we're here and hitting us with a saccharine smile. "Hey, guys!"

"Uhh, everything okay?" Mav asks.

"Oh," she snorts. "Yeah. That was Netflix. Did you know they raised their pricing again? Nineteen dollars a month. And for what? I've barely even watched it since they cancelled Orange is the New Black."

I furrow my brows in confusion, opting to keep my mouth shut. It's for my own good.

"Anyway," she says, sitting down in her luxurious leather chair. "Let's talk about that breakup."

Maverick stiffens, reaching over to grab my hand. "Twyla, I already told you. I love Bella. We are in love. We're not breaking up."

Confusion clouds her expression for a moment, and I feel sweat start to bead on the back of my neck. I knew she'd be mad at us for throwing her plan out the window. I hope she doesn't yell at us like she did poor Sharon.

We sit, staring at each other for another thirty seconds before she busts out laughing. "You guys," she heaves between snorts. "I'm fucking with you. I knew you'd end up together for real."

I scrunch my nose as she uses her fingers to carefully tap away the tears of laughter making their way down her face. "You what?" I ask, not absorbing her words quick enough.

She takes a breath, composing herself. "Bella, for ten years, I've watched you do everything you were told. You never ask for anything, and nobody gives your wants or needs a second thought. And Maverick," she says, moving her eyes to him. "You were letting life pass you by, only focusing on football and being the best. I knew you were too stubborn to go find love on your own. So, I gave you both a little nudge. I knew you'd be the perfect partners for one another."

I choke out a laugh, not even sure what the right reaction should be. On one hand, I feel like I should be pissed that she meddled in my personal life. But, then again, that meddling brought me to Maverick, so can I really be mad?

Mav exhales beside me, his eyebrows nearly kissing his hairline. "Wow."

Yeah, that's a good enough reaction. "Wow is right," I echo him.

She just gives us a smug smile as she wipes imaginary dust from her desk. "You know, you *could* say thank you."

Maverick stands up, offering his hand for her to shake. She obliges. "Thank you, Twyla, for putting your nose where it didn't belong. If you hadn't, I'd have never met the future mother of my children. But going forward, please, for the love of God, stay out of our business." A vision of me, holding a little version of him pulls me away from reality for just a moment before I stand up, grabbing his hand again.

She puts her hands up in surrender. "You have my word. Now, get out of my office."

We do just that, heading toward the elevator and into whatever adventure life brings our way next.

EPILOGUE

MAVERICK

"DO YOU HAVE THE GIFT?" I ask Bella as we step out of the car and head down the walkway to Dalton's new home.

"Yep," she answers, holding up the bottle of wine and gift card we brought as a housewarming present. When Dalton told us he bought this house on a whim a couple weeks ago, we were all shocked that he was moving out of his bachelor pad in the city. But the guy is pretty much a loose cannon one hundred percent of the time, so we all just went with it.

Bella rings the doorbell, and I take the opportunity to grab her and drop my lips to hers. Our kiss turns frenzied in an instant, and by the time the door opens, I have her pushed against one of the pillars on the porch with my hand running up the back of her thigh as she moans into my mouth.

"Good fucking God," Dalton groans from the doorway. "Could you two please not fuck on my front lawn? I have neighbors." He peeks around to see if anyone is looking as we walk past him into the house like two teenagers getting scolded by their dad.

Mads chimes in. "Oh, they can't kiss outside of *your house*, but you can bang the Playmate of the Year on the patio table outside ours?" Blaze chuckles as he pulls her into his lap at the kitchen table.

Dalton scoffs. "First of all, she was Miss December. Secondly, nobody asked you to check the security footage like you're heading the goddamn FBI, Shorty."

"If you must know, you walking herpes medication ad, I was trying to spy on Blaze. Sometimes he skinny dips out there and I wanted to see his dick," she says with a shrug.

Blaze looks at his girlfriend, feigning offense. "Baby Doll, if you wanted to see the big, bad monster, all you had to do was ask." She goes to argue, but he grabs her cheeks roughly between his thumb and fingers and smacks a kiss on her smooshed lips, silencing her.

Tanner throws his head back in a laugh from his chair in the corner. He was being so quiet; I didn't even know he was here. That's very on-brand for him. He's still the most mysterious motherfucker I know.

"Anyway," Dalton says, standing in front of us. "Thank you all for coming. I wanted to make sure all the most important people in our lives were here today."

Our? What is he talking about?

He looks over at Dia, who puts her chin up, walks over to stand beside him, and links her hand with his. The entire group collectively gasps as they smile at one another before looking back at us.

"We have something to tell you."

ACKNOWLEDGMENTS

My husband - I can't say it enough…this book wouldn't exist without you. Your confidence in my ability to do anything makes me just delulu enough to go for it every time. I'm forever grateful that you chose me. I love you infinity.

My kids - Again, if you ever read any of my books, you're grounded.

My mom - You've given me so much courage on this journey. When I was worried about what people might think, you told me they didn't matter. I can't tell you how important that was for me to hear. Thank you for always having the right words. I hope I continue to make you proud.

Breanne at Breezy Book Edits - I couldn't be prouder of you. Deciding that you want to make a change in your life isn't easy, but you're doing it so enthusiastically that it just inspires me to work that much harder at my own stuff. This is *our journey* and I wouldn't want to do it with anyone else. Here's to many more books in our future!

Hannah Gray - You have given me the courage to do so many things I never thought I'd do. When I get discouraged, you never hesitate to drop what you're doing to talk me off the ledge. You're the very first person who referred to me as "an author" and I don't think I'll ever forget the impact that had on me. I love you to the moon and I'm so grateful for your friendship.

Lexi James - My friend, my sister, my carbon copy. Nobody relates to me the way you do and that has changed my life. I know if I need to work through something, you're just about thirty consecutive voice messages away. You always seem to know what I need to hear to get me right back on track. I couldn't write a damn word of this stuff without you. Love you to bits!

Amanda Mudgett - Thank you for loving my characters as much as I do. Whenever I think something sucks, you're the first one to hype me up and get me out of my own head. You've become such an important part of my process…never leave me or I'll stalk you and make you love me forever.

Jenn and Nicole - We did it again, girls! Your encouragement and input mean the world to me. Thank you for coming on this journey with me!

My beta and ARC readers - I still can't find words to express my gratitude. I don't think I'll ever be able to thank you for your continued support. You truly are the best.

My readers - I hope you loved Maverick and Bella. Their story wasn't one I planned to write, but your encouragement made me want to give you the best novella I possibly could. Thank you for being a part of this with me!

Nick Bosa - Uhhhh…thanks for being cute as fuck. And for being the perfect inspo for Maverick.

ABOUT THE AUTHOR

C.L. Rose is a wife and mother of two. She lives in Northeast Ohio with her husband, son, daughter, and dog, Tank. When she isn't writing, you can find her reading in front of a space heater, wrapped in a thick blanket, probably complaining that she's cold.

◎ ♪ ⑫

MORE FROM THE BOSTON BLIZZARD SERIES

Printed in Poland
by Amazon Fulfillment
Poland Sp. z o.o., Wrocław